...JNE 2

– Written by –

CARYN LEE

Copyright © 2014 by Royal Dynasty Publications
Published by Royal Dynasty Publications LLC
First Edition

Facebook:
https://www.facebook.com/caryndeniselee?fref=ts

Cover design/Graphics: Michael Horne

Editor: /Tiffany Stephens

ACKNOWLEDGEMENTS I would like to thank God for everything. You have opened doors for me that I never even imagined were there to be opened. Thank you for opening up my eyes and allowing me to see a vision that I didn't know was there. I praise you for that. I'd like to thank my family and friends for supporting and promoting my debut novel Blackbone. You all rock and I love each and every one of you! Finally I would love to thank all my readers. You play a very important role. Thank you for all your reviews, emails, and for supporting me as well! I appreciate you all! Keep it coming!

Chapter 1

Smooth

The ambulance driver sped through the traffic. Ciara was unconscious, but the baby still had a heart beat.

"Ciara baby stay with me and Eric J. I'm sorry baby we need you." I said.

The paramedics were able to get a pulse. Once we got inside they rushed her into the emergency room. I wasn't allowed to go to the back with her. I called my mother, Jasmine, Kelly, Vell, Ant, and Red. They all rushed up there.

"Where is she?" Jasmine asked.

"She's in the back." I said.

"What happened, Smooth?" Kelly asked.

"She's alright." I said.

I didn't bother to tell them what happened. Everyone else got there, and we were waiting in the ER for an hour until the doctor came in. We all stood up.

"Are you the family of Ciara Robinson?" The doctor asked.

"Yes, is she ok?"

"She's stable. We had to perform an emergency cesarean due to Ms. Robinson's blood pressure being extremely high. The baby boy is fine. He weighs 5lbs, so we have to observe him closely. However, Ms. Robinson has lost a lot of blood, so we had to give her a blood transfusion." The doctor said.

"Why is the baby so small, is he premature?" Jasmine asked.

"No it is typically normal for a baby to weigh 5lbs to 5.5lbs during 37 to 40 weeks. That is what we consider a low weight birth. With plenty of nutrition we will help the baby get up to a healthy weight," said the doctor.

"When can we see Ciara and the baby?" I asked.

"Ms. Robinson is resting now, but I will allow you to see her for twenty minutes. You can see the baby in the nursery." The doctor said.

We all rushed in the room. Ciara was in the bed sleeping. She had on an oxygen mask, tubes running in and out of her arms, and the bag of blood was hanging from the pole. My mother said a prayer as we all prayed over her. One by one everyone kissed Ciara. Jasmine took it the hardest. Kelly stared at me like she wanted to kick my ass. Vell, Ant, and Red showed me love before leaving.

Everyone left me in the room alone with Ciara. I cried as I looked at my woman lying in the hospital bed.

"Look what I caused. Ciara I love you and I'm so sorry. I promise to be there for you and Eric Jr. I never meant for this to happen. I will never leave your side again. I can't live if something ever happened to you. I love you baby," I pleaded, and even tried to pay the doctor to allow me to stay overnight, but he didn't let me stay.

I kissed Ciara and went to the nursery to go see my son. He was tiny and had dark skin just like me and his mom. The nurses didn't have to tell me who my baby was, I knew right away. Eric Jr. had tubes running in him as well. Immediately I felt bad for putting his mother through so much stress. He wasn't ready to be born. It was my entire fault due to the double life that I was living, and it was starting to catch up with me. I felt bad for everything I was doing. Hiding another baby, which is my daughter and sleeping with Rochelle and Kayla. I had to get back focused on my home.

Ciara

Where am I? I looked around and noticed I was in a hospital room. I saw balloons, flowers, cards, and there were machines beeping. I looked down at my belly and grabbed my stomach. I was no longer pregnant.

"My baby! Where's my baby?" I screamed.

I tried to get up, but I fell to the floor. The nurses ran into the room.

"What's going on and where is my baby?"

"Ms. Robinson calm down and relax. You're in the hospital." The nurse said.

"Where the fuck is my baby?"

"Your baby is fine, he's in the nursery. You passed out at home and you had to get an emergency cesarean."

I lifted up my gown to look at my belly. It looked like it had been cut.

"I want to see my baby right now! Please can I have my son?!" I cried.

"Yes, I will bring your son as soon as I finish your vitals."

The nurse had to check my vitals and examine my body because I hit the floor. Once everything was fine she left the room to go get my baby. Fifteen minutes later she came into my room. I sat up in bed so that I could hold my son.

"Here is your son Eric Jr.", the nurse said.

"Oh my you look just like your father." I cried.

I let the tears fall and asked the nurse why my baby was so small.

"You didn't finish your full term of pregnancy Ciara. Are you going to breast feed?" Asked the nurse.

"Yes, I am." I said.

"Okay I will have the nurse come in and instruct you on how to breast feed."

The nurse left the room. I took off Eric Jr.'s hat and he had a head full of black hair. I checked to see if he had all his fingers and toes. I even checked his wee wee. My Lil Man had been circumcised. I kissed him on his forehead.

Twenty minutes later Smooth ran in the room, scaring me and Eric Jr.

"Ciara baby you up, I came as soon as they called me."

I rocked Eric Jr. to calm him down.

"Where you been Smooth?" I asked with a slight attitude.

"I had to go handle some business."

"Still handling business I see."

"It's not what you think Ciara."

Smooth started to explain but the doctor walked in.

"Hello Ms. Robinson, how are you?"

"I'm fine." I said.

"That's great you gave us all a scare young lady. Your blood pressure was dangerously high; we could not get it to go down without harming the baby. Therefore we had to perform an emergency cesarean. During that surgery you lost a lot of blood and we had to give you a blood transfusion. I see you have met you son. Do you mind giving him to his dad for a minute so that I can examine you?"

Smooth took Eric Jr.

"When can I go home?" I asked.

"Maybe in three days. We just need to make sure that everything is fine before you leave." The doctor said.

"Can I please have something to eat?" I asked.

"I will put you on a clear liquid diet, and if you do well with that, I will change you to a regular diet."

"Okay that's fine with me." I said.

"Do you have any more questions?"

"No, not at the moment."

"If you do, have the nurse to page me I will be in the hospital until 8 p.m. Congratulations you two." The doctor said.

He left the room leaving us some privacy. Smooth laid Eric Jr. down. I was trying to find something on television to watch. The room was quiet, so Smooth broke the silence.

"Ciara I'm sorry about everything." He said.

I stopped him from talking.

"Not now Smooth. I just want to focus on the future. If you want to keep fucking up that's on you. Eric Jr. is priority now, and he's all that matters. I'm a mother now, so he becomes first. I don't have time for the extra bullshit. I love you Smooth, but if you ever decide that you want to leave, the door is open. I'm not making no man stay where he don't want to be."

"Ciara I love you. What the fuck you mean if I want to leave the door is opened? You and Eric Jr. are the most important people in my life. You are my Queen and that's my Prince. No one could ever come between that. I know I fucked up and I'm sorry. But you not going anywhere, we in this shit forever Blackbone. I promise to start being more family orientated. I'm going to get you that house and make you my wife. No more staying out late I'm tired of the fighting and arguing. After what happened last week, I realized how much I love you and don't ever want to lose you."

I wanted to believe Smooth, but I didn't. Right now love was the last thing on my mind. It was time for me to work on being a good mother instead of a good girlfriend. My room phone rang and I answered it, but it was someone with the wrong number. The phone ringing woke up the baby. Smooth picked him up and got in the bed with me. We were bonding with our baby then there was a knock on the door.

"Come in", we both said.

It was the nurse who was teaching me how to breast feed. Right on time Eric Jr. was hungry. It hurt like hell and was uncomfortable. My baby was sucking on my nipples hard. He was starving. Once the nurse felt that I was ready, she left the room. I pumped milk into his bottles, burped my baby and Smooth changed his diaper.

Hours later everyone was in the room, Jasmine and Shawn were on the IPad face timing us. They couldn't be here because they were on a cruise. Ms. Jackson couldn't stop taking pictures of her grandson. Kelly helped me get pretty and bought me some clothes from my boutique to wear. I wanted to look good in the pictures; Vell bought me something to eat. I was starving for some real food. Ms. Jackson warned me to watch what I ate, because I was breast feeding. Anything that I ate my son could taste it in his breast milk. I took that in mind, but right now I was maxing.

Two hours went by, and finally everyone had left. Smooth stayed overnight and was in the chair snoring with Junior lying on his chest. I snapped a picture of that. I turned the television off and fell asleep.

"Take your time baby. I got you and not going to let you fall. Walk as slow as you can, take your time." Smooth said.

I went to the bathroom to take a shower. The C-section had me in a little pain. We finally made it to the bathroom and I was sitting on the toilet peeing while Smooth ran the water. I left the bathroom door open, just in case my baby started crying so that we can hear him. Removing the hospital gown I noticed the cut. It wasn't so bad because they gave me a bikini cut. Smooth help me shower, we had to be careful because I still had the stitches and I was sore. The water felt good against my back. Once I got out the shower, I put lotion on my body and slipped on a tunic and some leggings. We were sitting on the couch in the room when we heard a knock on the door.

"Housekeeping, can I come in to clean the room?"

"Yes, its cool", Smooth said.

I was busy preparing myself to feed Eric Jr. The housekeeper came inside and I completely froze.

"Ciara baby is that you", she said.

Smooth just looked back and forth at the both of us.

Brenda

"Oh my God, Ciara baby it's really you,"

I dropped the broom and supplies and ran over to hug my daughter.

"Thank you Jesus", I cried.

She was so beautiful. At first she hesitated a little bit, but after a second she hugged me back.

"Mama, you're alive", Ciara said.

"Yes, baby why would you think that I was dead?"

"Because I came back looking for you everywhere, and no one seemed to know where you were,"

We embraced and hugged I didn't want to let her go ever again.

"You're so beautiful", I said as I gave her so many kisses.

"Oh my God I miss you so much and I prayed every night for this reunion,"

"I'm so sorry baby; I've never met to hurt you. It was the alcohol. I let it take over my life. The devil had control over me, but not anymore. I've been clean for more than a year now. I got myself together. After you were taken away my life spiraled down. I lost everything and I had to go live in a women's shelter. There I got help with my alcohol addiction. It was a 12 week program, it was hard, but I finished it. They also helped me find a place and job. I came back looking for you too, but by that time you were discharged. Look at how beautiful you've grown up to be,"

"Thank you Mama", Ciara cried.

"It's ok to cry baby", I said as I wiped away Ciara tears.

I looked over at the young man holding the baby and then back at Ciara.

"That's Eric my boyfriend Mama, and that's my son Eric Jr.,"

"Hello Eric, nice to meet you, I'm Ciara's mother, Brenda Robinson,"

"Hello Ms. Robinson. Can I hold my Grandson? You know what, never mind, I can't

I'm on the clock and have on this nasty uniform. I get off at 7 p.m., would it be ok if I came back after work?"

Ciara paused for a minute and looked over at her boyfriend. He nodded his head.

"Sure you can Mama,"

I cleaned up her room and ran my mouth the entire time is was in there.

"Okay baby I'm done here. I will be back once I get off. I spent long enough in here let Mama finish her job before I get wrote up,"

"Okay mama, but you looked funny. I've never seen you clean up before", Ciara laughed.

"Oh hush child", I laughed as I left her alone to clean the rest of my rooms.

During the rest of the day, I couldn't even concentrate on my job. I called her room to talk to her on my lunch break as I was eating. We caught up on as much as we could in forty-five minutes. I couldn't wait to meet her two best friends, and get to know her boyfriend. He seemed like a respectable man. I'm so happy that Ciara wasn't angry and shut me out of her life. Our last encounter was us fighting and her being sent away. 7:00 p.m. couldn't come fast enough. I hurried up to change my clothes went back to visit Ciara. When I made it back to her room, there was an older woman there. I assumed it was Eric's mother since he looked just like her.

"Hello, I'm Brenda Robinson, Ciara's mother", I spoke.

She stood up and introduced herself as Ms. Jackson, Eric's mother.

"Nice to meet you,"

"How was your day Mama?" Ciara asked.

"It was busy, but fine!"

"Have a seat", Eric said.

I sat down and held my grandson. It felt odd that I was given the chance to become a mother again, and happy I was also becoming a grandmother as well.

Jasmine

Vegas was live and I was so happy that Shawn took the time out to take me. We needed to get away from the drama in Chicago. With all the things that are going on, I don't know how much longer I was going to remain calm. I really didn't feel comfortable being here right after my best friend just had her baby. After all Ciara had her baby early and I don't think that anyone was expecting that. I was very upset with Smooth ass and wanted to smack the shit out of him. Anyway I'm going to leave all that bullshit back in Chicago and enjoy Vegas. Shawn and I were staying at Bellagio. It was beautiful as soon as we walked inside. It was so many people walking around. We made it to our hotel in the am. The door man helped us with our bags. We checked in at the desk and he assisted us until with got to our room. Shawn tipped him and I walked inside We had a Bellagio Suite. It was spacious with marble floors and a luxurious king size bed. I kicked off my shoes and walked around the suite to check out everything. Shawn was opened the blinds and admiring the view. I walked up to him and he wrapped his arms around me.

"The view is beautiful Shawn. I'm so happy to be here in Vegas with you." I said.

"Anything for you sweetheart. Besides we needed a break and I can handle some business too while I'm down here." Shawn said.

"Wait what do you mean by handling business? Shawn you promise me that it was only going to be about me and you." I said.

"Baby I know but I called one of my partners from Cali and told him to meet me here. I felt that I would be cool so that I wouldn't have to make the trip for Cali next month." Shawn said.

"It's fine bae. I know how you have to make your money. I'm going to soak in the whirlpool. Do you care to join me?" I asked.

"Hell yeah! Bae let's get started." Shawn said.

I went to go run the water in the whirlpool. I took off all my clothes and walked around the suite naked. The blinds were still opened. I walked over to the big glass window and exposed my naked ass body. Shawn smiled and watched. He turned on the radio and 'Diced Pineapples' came on. I danced slowly to the music. I rolled my body and sang' "Call me crazy but at least you call me." I walked over to Shawn and kissed hi softly on the lips.

"I love you Jas" Shawn said.
"I love you too." I whispered in his ear.

I licked his ear lope and took him by the hand and walked to the whirlpool. We got inside, I straddled on top of him. I gasped when Shawn slid inside me. I bounced up and down on his dick as he sucked my breast.

"Oh yes Shawn. You feel so good inside me." I moaned.

"I'm loving this pussy Jas." Shawn said.

I rode him and I felt my orgasm coming. I wrapped my arms around him. Shawn held me and we both tongue kissed. He was about to nut and started grabbling my hair and neck. We were soaking wet as water dripped down our face.

Chapter2
THREE MONTHS LATER…
Ciara

"Smooth can you warm up the baby's milk, please? Eric Jr. is in a cranky mood and won't stop crying,"

I checked his temperature and it was normal. Smooth bought the bottle to me. I fed and burped him, but he was still whining. I called up both my mother and Smooth's mother for some help. Ms. Jackson came over; my Mother was at work and couldn't make it. Ms. Jackson volunteered to take Eric Jr. for a few days. I wasn't saying no to that, I needed a break. I was blessed to have a mother-in-law like that. I kissed my baby goodbye and he was off to be with his grandma. The house was quiet and I was so happy to be baby free. Don't get me wrong I love my baby, but I was starting to get depressed. Jasmine and Kelly called me and we decided to step out tonight. Smooth didn't mind and besides I need some excitement.

They arrived at my place around 10 p.m. Kelly was pushing Anthony's Range Rover. We all went to Billboard Live and it was crazy packed. We had a table in VIP. I, Jasmine, and Kelly stepped in that bitch and all eyes were on us. We looked good. I had on my all black one shoulder Givenchy dress with my black Tom Ford Boots. Kelly had on a custom made dress by Queen Russia, and a pair of black sling back Christian Louboutin. Jasmine rocked a bad ass all black jumpsuit from BCBG, with a pair of black BCBG pumps. The music was blasting, we ordered a few bottles, but I only drank water though. I wasn't drinking, but that didn't stop Jasmine's and Kelly's flow. The DJ was on point tonight. Jeezy's "RIP" bumped through the speakers.

"That's my shit", I got up and started dancing.

I didn't come out to look pretty, I came out to party. We danced to Jeezy as everyone watched us. The hoes hated, but the niggas loved it. Shawn came through with a couple of his buddies.

"Hey Bro", I said as I gave him a hug.

"What's good sis?" He said.

He walked over to Jasmine. After a few more songs I finally stop dancing and sat my ass down. Going in my clutch I pulled out my cell phone and I had several text messages from Smooth. He was saying that he was going to slide through. I showed Kelly the text message because I knew Anthony was going to be with him.

Smooth, Ant, Vell, and Red slid through the party. They bought more bottles. I danced on my man to every song. We snapped a few pictures and left. After that we rode to Greek Town to get us some chicken on pitas. I drove back home because Smooth was drunk.

Smooth was fucked up, but he kept saying he was cool. I undressed him and myself and started sucking his dick. He laid back and enjoyed it. It had been a minute since I've gave him some head. I was still holding a slight grudge against him. I sucked until his busted a nut and kept on sucking. He pulled me on top of him and I started to ride his dick. I was going in slow motion; he grabbed one of my breasts and started sucking on my nipples. His dick fell good inside me. Riding his dick I was in control and Smooth enjoyed every bit of the way I was rotating my hips. His drunken ass was talking crazy and saying all types of shit. I laughed. I kissed his drunken ass and put my tongue down his throat.

"I love you baby", I said. I came all over his dick, fell out on his chest and went to sleep

The next morning I woke up to an empty bed. I got up to go shower. I heard Smooth come back in with some breakfast. I called to check on my baby and he was doing much better. We ate and discussed when we were going to move into a house. Smooth made a few phone calls and we were able to go and look at some places today. I was excited because I always wanted a family home. I came from court way buildings. Don't get me wrong downtown is the shit. But you can't raise a child downtown. I got dressed and we went to look at a four places in the western suburbs. I liked two and decided on one. We did the paperwork and we were looking forward to moving. Smooth dropped me back off at the house and I took a quick nap. I got up to my phone ringing. It was London calling me from the boutique. I made a run up there to order some things and to help with the new inventory. I had plans on expanding my boutique; I wanted my new location to be bigger. The day went by fast and London and I knocked everything out.

I made it home by 9 p.m. I called Smooth, but he didn't answer. He came strolling in right before 12 a.m., I was in the bed watching television.

"I miss my baby, are you going to pick up Junior tomorrow?" Smooth asked.

"Yes, I am, I called earlier today and told her that I will be by there at noon. Then from there, I'm spending time with my mother. We didn't have any plans tomorrow, did we?" I asked.

"No, we don't babe", Smooth said as he gave me a kiss.

"I'm tired babe; I'm going to bed,"

He got in the bed with me and he fell asleep. I knew that he must have been fucking because he didn't try to have sex with me. The next morning Smooth and I fucked. I was out the house by noon to get my son from Smooth's mother. I made my way to my mother's house in K town. She was happy that I was spending the day with her. She cooked dinner and was happy that she could see Junior.

"I'm happy that you two came to visit me today. I miss my grandbaby. I've been working so much. I'm trying to save up to get a car. I know you getting tired of driving me around. Anyway, how is everything going on at home?"

"I've been meaning to come by and spend some time with you. We have a lot of catching up to do. As far as me, everything is fine and I'm getting used to becoming a mother. At first I was afraid and didn't know what to do. You know I wasn't expecting to be a young mother, but I wouldn't trade Eric Junior for nothing in the world. Smooth and I are fine, but at times I want to kill him. We went to look at some houses today and I picked out one. I'm just ready to move. You know something bigger. The other day at the boutique I thought about finding a better location, everything seems so crowded,"

"It sounds like you need some space. Having a baby can be a little over whelming at times. Having a child makes you want more out of life. Makes you want to grow up. That's how I was when I first found out I was pregnant with you. I was so happy until,"

"Until what Mama, why did you stop talking?" I said.

"You can talk to me now about it. I'm no longer a little girl I'm a grown woman now. You were going to say something about my father. What about him? Is he the reason why you starting drinking?"

"Your father had a real bad gambling problem. He would bet on anything. That caused us to have a lot of debt. He was stressed out and he used to beat me when I stop supporting his habit. One day, he owed some people money or else they were going to kill him. It was on a Friday night, I had just got paid and went to bingo and won some money. Returning home, your father was waiting for me to give him some money. I refused and we fought and argued. He beat me repeatedly until I gave up the money. I ran inside the room and locked the door. He kicked the door in and entered. I took the gun out of the closet and shot him. He grabbed his chest and fell to the floor. I killed him Ciara. I was tired of all the gambling, beatings, and hiding my money. I called the police and told them that some people beat me and killed my husband because he owed them money. Everyone knew that your father was a gambler. So the police never questioned me or assumed I was lying. After that I was alone and pregnant. I had you and it was hard doing it alone. I lost my job because I couldn't afford to pay anyone to watch you. I had to get on public assistance. I was getting food stamps and a check. I was depressed and turned to alcohol and start drinking. I'm sorry baby that I took my frustration out on you. I was dealing without a lot and had your father's death on my hands,"

I couldn't believe what I was hearing. I sat there and cried with my Mother. Right now I didn't want to blame her for the past. I wanted to move forward. We hugged one another and for the first time it were genuine and real.

"Please forgive me Ciara, but I didn't know what else to do,"

"It's ok Mama, you did what you felt what was best at the time to protect you and I. I'm just happy that you are back in my life and no longer drinking. Thanks for telling me the truth and giving me some closure. Do you have any pictures of him?" I asked my mother.

"I have a few,"

She went in her room and came out with a shoe box. She showed me some pictures of my father.

"Oh my, I'm the spitting image of him", I cried.

"Yes, that's was a bigger part of the reason why I took everything out on you. Every time I looked at you I saw him,"

I pulled his obituary out and read it. After that I hugged and forgave her. We ate and talked about the many other relatives that I have. It was getting late and Smooth kept calling my phone so I decided to leave. My mother kissed me and her grandson good bye. I left and I felt like a weight was lifted off my shoulder.

Rochelle

Smooth came by to visit baby Erica and sat me down to have a talk.

"We can't sleep together anymore. I went too far when I did that with you. My priority is my baby girl and when we fight, the focus isn't on her. I will always be her father and do my part, but me and you Rochelle will never be together again,"

"I'm not asking to be with you so don't flatter yourself. Admit that you wanted to sleep with me just as much as I wanted to sleep with you. Hell you might want to fuck me right now; if we fuck or not, I'm still cool with you. You're a good father and I felt that you deserved the pussy, but if you want to stop fucking me then understand. What do you expect to happen when you come over and spend hours over here?"

Walking past Smooth with my tank and leggings on, I watched his eyes scan my body. He couldn't resist this. I was thicker than a snicker. I wasn't trying to hear that bullshit he was talking about. I wanted to see how long he could go without sleeping with me. I guess with Ciara having her baby he was starting to feel some type of way. I really don't care about her baby as long as he doesn't forget about baby Erica. I walked back in the room and Smooth was talking on the phone. I can tell by the conversation that it was

Ciara. After the phone call Smooth had to go and handle some business. He kissed baby Erica and told her that Daddy will be back.

"Excuse me where you going so fast? You haven't been here to see your daughter in two weeks. You come to visit her less than an hour and you get a phone call from Ciara and you have to leave. Every time Ciara calls you take off running. Fuck that, Baby Erica needs your time as well!"

"I have to go and handle some business I will be right back. Give me an hour I promise!"

He left jumped in his car and sped off. It's been two hours, and just like I expected he didn't come back. Smooth didn't show up or call. The next day came and left and so did the next week. I called several times, but he didn't or returns my calls. I was done and fed the fuck up; no more of me reaching out to man who doesn't want to be involved in my daughter's life. Fuck Smooth, and when he is ready to come back around, the shit wasn't going to be easy. Just like he was always busy, so would I be busy. It was time to give him a taste of his own medicine. I was so angry that I wanted to go downtown and ring his doorbell and tell her all about Baby Erica. Then the bitch would know where her man has been spending all his time. I noticed the family pictures that we took. A light bulb went off in my head.

Chapter 3
Ciara

I was finally moving inside my new home. We were moving to Westchester. In a three bedrooms, two full bathrooms, and a finished basement, plus a two car garage. Boxes were everywhere. Smooth had his people from his Moving Company provide their services. The movers were doing a great job. I pretty much directed them how I wanted things done. Eric Junior was with his grandma. Smooth was running back and forth and didn't pretty much help at all. He felt that he paying for it was his workers. Eight hours later they were done. They put the dining room furniture together and the bedroom sets. I was so happy that I only had to do the minimum, and that was unpacking the things in the kitchen and a few of my clothes and shoes.

I was soaking inside the Jacuzzi tub and Smooth went to go make a food run. I relaxed and let my mind drift off. Smooth scared the hell out of me. I had drifted off to sleep and he tapped me to wake me up. I screamed and jumped.

"Are you having another nightmare?"

"No, you scared me,"

I got out the tub and dried off. He bought some from Chipotle's. I was starving and I devoured the food.

"You know what you want to do for your 21st birthday?" Smooth asked me.

"No, I'm not sure yet. Maybe I will throw a birthday dinner, you know, do something private; only inviting my closest family and friends, nothing too big,"

I went on and on about what I wanted to do. After a while Smooth tuned me out and I was pretty much talking to myself. He fell asleep on me. I excused it because we did have a very long day due to all the moving. I cleaned up the food mess and joined my man in bed.

The next day I unpacked my clothes, and believe it or not Smooth helped me out. We had the music playing and we were acting silly dancing and playing. We were done with everything by 2 p.m.

"Baby can I have some company?" Smooth asked.

I laughed and said, "Yes, you can have company!"

Vell, Red, and Ant came over and they all went down to the basement. That was his place and

I was fine with it. Smooth had our old sectional setup down there, with a 60 inch TV with surround sound, and a pool table. It also has a kitchen area and a bathroom.

"Baby I'm about step out and run a few errands,"

He ran upstairs and gave me a hug and a kiss. I tasted the Patron and weed on his tongue.

"You cool baby, you need any cash?" He asked.

"Well, I can use some cash,"

He gave me a few bills and I was on my way. It was a rainy spring day, but not in my world. All I saw was sunshine. I went by Kelly's place and kicked it with her.

"Hey, what's up? How's the new place? We gonna have to have a sleep over next month girl", Kelly said.

"It's nice we are done with everything and Smooth and the fellas are at the house in the basement now. They sipping and smoking that basement out girl,"

"Girl, let me fill you up on the gossip. So you know Rich is Ebony's baby daddy, girl. He got the DNA test done and he the baby daddy. I heard they suppose to live together and everything somewhere out south. That's crazy she with her best friend's man,"

"Get the fuck out of here. What Shunda say I know she gonna beat the fuck out that girl, I feel sorry for her. That's a shame because now their children are brother and sister. Rich need to be embarrassed. That shit ain't cool and what do you tell your children?"

"Half of these niggas ain't shit out here. I heard he fucked up too. Ant said he seen him the other day at the gas station in Ebony's car on Austin and Jackson looking rough. That's what happens when you fuck with bum bitches with no hustle. I remember when he was locked up for that year and Shunda worked two jobs; one to take care of her and the children, and the other one to keep money on Rich's books and the phone. She was down for her man. Ebony not gonna lift a finger for that nigga. He gonna find out,"

"So now you have Ant all to yourself. No baby mama drama. I know you happy that you don't have to deal with Ebony's crazy ass. Hell, I know Ant's happy he ain't the daddy. That would have been a fucking headache. Do you think you would have been able to be with him if he was the father of Ebony's child?"

"No, that would have destroyed our relationship. I wouldn't trust him around her hoe ass. She would've made her pussy available to him every day. Ant would have fucked her again. Let's be honest, she is an attractive girl. As soon as he would have fucked her, she would throw it back in my face. Plus, he would have got her a place and everything just because he is that type of nigga. That's why she wanted him to be her baby daddy in the first place. I wasn't going to sit back, be the girlfriend, and watch that shit. Besides, I don't have to deal with that shit. I don't have any kids, I have my own cash, car, and crib. Anthony would have been kicked to the left without a problem. Enough about me; when are you going to let me keep my nephew?"

"When you want to? Junior been keeping me busy he getting bigger too. Smooth be having him watching sports with him. You should see it; Smooth be drinking a beer and Baby Smooth be drinking his bottle. Girl he's a mini version of his daddy it's so scary. I'm not surprised that he looks like him because I stayed hating Smooth during my pregnancy,"

"Yes, sister, he almost got fucked up at the hospital. Anthony told me to be cool. He was lucky because, if it wasn't for him, Smooth wouldn't have got it that night. I just my stayed my distance from him. I know he was stressing you out and shit. I'm just happy to see that everything is back to normal. But if it happens again, I'm not sparing him. I'm going upside his head. I'm laughing but you know I'm so fucking serious." Kelly said.

"I know, Sis, and I will do the same for you. You coming outside today? Let's go up to the shop with Jasmine. Let me call her up." I said.

"What's up I'm at Kelly's place we about to slide in on you." I said to Jasmine.

"Bring me a polish from Abe and Tommie's." Jasmine said.

"Bitch you greedy we not bringing you shit to eat." I said laughing.

"Come on fareal don't be like that!"

"Okay, be there in thirty minutes." I said then hung up.

"She talking about stop by Abe and Tommie's and grab a polish." I told Kelly.

We pulled up on Chicago Avenue and Leclaire and went inside the restaurant. I ordered the food and spoke to all my people. We left out, and as we were walking to the car I noticed my car was scratched up.

"What the fuck?!" I said as I dropped the motherfucking food and walked around my car to look at it. I looked around to see who was standing outside. There wasn't a person in sight. I was pissed. I pulled out my phone and called Smooth. He told me to meet him up at the shop. I listened to Kelly talk and she asked me if Smooth was still cheating on me. He may be who knows it could have been one of his silly ass hoes. Only hating bitches scratch up cars. I called Jasmine and told her what happened. She asked me the same thing, if it was someone Smooth was fucking with. I didn't know who it was, but when I found out she was getting cutting up. That was a coward ass move. I was pissed.

"Kelly why this bitch playing with me. She don't know my background but I see she is dying to find out. She fucked with wrong one!" I said.

I was flying down the street. When I got to the shop they worked on my car. Smooth got up there fifteen minutes later. He went to look at. We went inside the office of the shop.

"Smooth who you fucking with? Don't lie to me! One of your little bitches gonna get fucked up!"

"Chill out Ciara. I don't know who did it but I promise I'm not fucking around on you." Smooth said.

I didn't say shit else but I wasn't going to find shit out from him. I had to do my own investigating. I didn't have time for this shit, but obviously this bitch had a problem with me. I left out the office and hollered at Kelly. She was down for whatever. Smooth dropped Kelly off and we rode back home in silence. I didn't have shit else to say about it. I was mad, but I wasn't going to let her fuck up my day.

"Go pick up the baby. I just want to see my baby right now. I just want to be with him now!" I said to Smooth.

We stopped by his mother's house and picked up Eric Junior. Ms. Williams sensed something was wrong, but I told her that I was fine. She talked to Smooth in private. I left the house, and me and the baby waited for him in the car. I felt like Smooth was doing something behind my back and was trying to cover the shit up.

Chapter 4
Smooth

I don't know who scratched up Ciara's car. I felt like it was Rochelle. I haven't been responding to her lately. When we went to go pick Lil Smooth up from my mom's house, she told me that Rochelle had called her crying. Saying that I haven't been to see my daughter and that I won't answer her calls. She feels as though my son is more important, and that I'm treating him better. She threatens to tell Ciara about the baby Erica. My mother encouraged me to talk to Ciara about the situation. She feels as though Ciara would want to know about it. I felt otherwise and still wasn't ready to confess. Ciara rode in silence in the car and once we got inside she remained quiet. It was a stressful; no sex night. Every time I tried to touch her she would tell me not to touch her.

The next day I got up Ciara and Junior had already left the house. I called her phone but she didn't bother to answer. I went out to make a few runs and check on my money. I made a stop at the shop to check on Ciara's car and it was almost finished. While I was there Kayla called me.

"What's up Kayla?"

"Smooth you tell me what's up; why your girl outside my house ringing my doorbell and banging on my door and shit!"

"Who Ciara, are you serious? What the fuck is she doing there?"

"I don't know, but you need to get her. You know I can't call the police. She's outside my house with two other girls telling me to come out!"

"Don't go out there. Don't even answer the door. Don't call the police. I would be there in a minute", I said.

"Okay, bye and hurry the fuck up!"

"Fuck!"

I called Ciara and she answered.

"What your little girlfriend called. Yep, I'm outside her house now. Bitch, you busted, what you thought I wasn't going to find out!" Ciara said.

"Ciara get the fuck from over there now, fucking with that damn girl. I'm not fucking with her and she ain't done shit to you. Leave her alone,"

"So you are defending her now. You in love with this bitch" Smooth? You want to protect her!"

CRASH! I heard a glass break. Ciara was yelling and screaming.

"Bitch since you don't want to come out, I will come in there to get you!"

I heard screaming and yelling and then the phone hung up. I made it to Kayla's house and when I got there I saw a police car. I rode past the police car, but Ciara wasn't in the back of it. I called her phone several times, but she didn't answer. I called Kayla and she picked up and was crying.

"Kayla calm down and don't tell the police anything. I would take care of everything,"

I heard Kayla tell the police that she didn't want to press charges. Another called came in, it was Ciara.

"Hello where are you? Why you didn't answer the phone when I called you?"

"Bitch, I'm in the house where the fuck are you? Over your girlfriend's place playing Captain Save A Hoe!"

"Ciara quit playing with me. Watch your mouth before I fuck you up. I'm on my way home, so be there when I get there!"

"Bitch, fuck you!" Ciara said and hung up the phone.

I made it home and she was sitting on the bed like nothing happen. Junior was lying next to her. *Smack!* I hauled off and smacked her ass across the bed. She grabbed her face, looked at me and starting crying.

"I hate you, Smooth. You promised not to hurt me. You out here fucking rat bitches and shit, and you want to hit me. I fucking hate you!"

"I'm sorry Ciara, but I told you to watch your fucking mouth. You shouldn't be so disrespectful, come here let me see you face,"

"Don't fucking touch me. Get away from me. I hate you. Go with your girlfriend,"

Eric Junior started crying. Ciara leaped up and grabbed the baby and starting running. Junior was crying loud as hell. Damn, I didn't have time for this bullshit. I caught up with Ciara and grabbed her by the neck.

"Let me go Smooth," she swung her little arm.

"Chill out Ciara, stop acting silly and sit your ass down, because if my baby get hurt, I'm really gonna fuck you up!" She sat down still running her mouth. I shook her.

"Listen I'm not fucking with that girl. I use her place as my stash house. Now you went your ass over there acting crazy and shit. She wasn't the person who fucked with your car. So who ever told you that sent your dumb ass off,"

"Who was the person who fucked with my car then, Smooth, since you talking tell me that?"

"Look some crazy ass girl," I lied.

"Don't worry I will handle her. She won't be bothering you again."

"Smooth you said that shit when someone called your phone in the a.m. hours. You swear when you out late that you not doing shit. You keep fucking lying. I know you fucking her. It's cool you do you and watch me do me!"

"Ciara you not going to do shit unless you want me to beat your ass; don't go back over there fucking with that girl. What's wrong with you? Why you going over people house and shit anyway?"

"What the fuck you mean what's wrong with me; bitches fucking with my car and shit over your sorry ass. I'm minding my own business. They taking they anger out on me because they upset you!"

Ciara had a point there. She wasn't doing shit, I was the one out there fucking around on her with Kayla and Rochelle. She had the right to be mad and upset. I started a lot of bullshit that I had to clean up.

I tried to let myself inside Rochelle place, but my key wasn't working. The bitch changed the locks on me. I rang the bell.

"Who is it?" Rochelle asked.

"Bitch open up the door! You know who this is!"

She opened up the door with a grin on her face.

"What brings you by here?"

"Don't play dumb with me. Why scratch up Ciara's car?"

"I don't know what you're talking about. I wasn't out West today,"

"How do you know her car was out West?"

SMACK!

"Bitch, stop lying,"

She grabbed the side of her face and started laughing.

"Where the fuck is my daughter?" I walked in her room and she wasn't there.

"She's over my parent's house,"

I walked back into the living room.

"Rochelle why the fuck would you scratched up Ciara's car? What's wrong with you are you crazy?"

"I'm not crazy. You don't pay me or the baby any attention ever since you had your baby. You see me calling you and shit. I shouldn't have to blow up your phone. You know you have a daughter over here that will be one years old real soon. It shouldn't take me fucking up "Wifey" car to get your attention. But the shit worked didn't it, because you over here now,"

"I was getting to you. I didn't forget about my baby. I told you that I had to take care of some business. And why are you calling my mother putting her in this mess? You are only to contact her if it's about the baby,"

"News flash it is about the baby. Why you think I'm acting like this? I don't want you,"

"Well if you don't want me, why are you fucking with my girl car? If you don't want me, why is my baby not here? You knew I was coming over here after you did that goofy shit to my girl car. Why would you send my daughter to your parent's house? That's because you want me alone and to yourself. Look what you have on. You were waiting on me to come over,"

"So what Smooth, yes I want you. How do you think I feel? I have your child, and don't forget us starting back fucking. I miss you and I just want you to act like you care. I know we can't be a family, but when you are over here it feels like we are a family. Then you leave us and go back home to her and your son and forget about us,"

She started crying I went over to hug her.

"Look I will never forget about you and my daughter. You know the situation when you start dealing with me. Plus I make sure you and baby Erica is always straight and give you money,"

"It's not about the money. You act like I'm a broke bitch!"

"I didn't say you were. But you are crazy and if you keep acting up I will cut your ass off. I won't cut my baby off, but I will get rid of you. Please don't act like I can't either,"

"I'm sorry baby I won't act crazy again. I will leave her alone,"

She started unzipping my pants. She walked me to her couch and sat me down. She pulled my pants down and dropped to her knees. Her warm mouth felt good around my dick. I didn't bother to stop her. Ciara and I haven't fucked in two days. I need to release some frustration. I grabbed her head and said, "Suck that dick baby momma!"

Chapter 5
Jasmine

With all that crazy shit that was happening between Ciara and Smooth. I almost lost focus on Shawn and I. was still cool but I didn't trust his ass. He has been going back and forth to Cali a lot to handle business. That didn't bother me too much except for the fact that he never takes me with him. We bump heads a few times about my nasty attitude. So I've been trying to work on that. It's hard because I feel like Shawn is up to something. Shawn was out in the streets again. He knows that Mondays are my off days and that I love to spend them with him. Today I got occupied with helping Ciara beat up Smooth's girlfriend, but now that that drama is over I needed my man.

Lying down on the couch watching Belly and sipping Ciroc I thought about Shawn being out there in the streets. I've been so emotional lately; just crying for no damn reason. Last month I went to the doctor and he diagnosed me with depression. He prescribed me Prozac; ever since then I've been popping pills and drinking. When I did pop a pill I felt like I was on top of the world. Shawn noticed that something was strange. But I denied it and told him that he was crazy. He was worried and concerned about my excessive drinking. So I only drank when I was alone and he wasn't around.

I decided to call Shawn.

"Hello baby, what are you doing?"

"I'm sitting here watching *Belly* and thinking about you,"

"No I'm not drinking, when are you coming home? I'm horny and I need you right now,"

"An hour is too long. Ha Ha Ha. I can wait. Oh and one more thing. I love you,"

I went in the bathroom to freshen up. I pulled out my police officer uniform and handcuffs. I loved to role play. My phone rang and it was Shawn calling me back. I picked up.

"Hello", I said.

"Hello, hello His phone called me back by mistake,"

I overheard Shawn having a conversation with someone. I didn't hang up. I kept on listening.

"Why do you have to go? You always go running when she calls you, I was enjoying your company babe,"

"When Wifey calls I have to go running. I will be back to see you tomorrow. You just be here when I get back and keep my pussy tight,"

"I will, babe. This pussy is yours and nobody else. Are you still taking me to Cali with you?"

I knew Shawn was up to something. I know he better not take that bitch to Cali with him. Her voice sounds familiar. It sounds like I heard it from somewhere before. They continued to talk and I heard the phone moving around.

"Nisha you seen my watch, help me find my watch. I will let you know if I'm still going to Cali or not,"

"Okay babe and here goes your watch. Call me when you can. I love you,"

Shawn didn't say anything back. I heard him get inside his car. Then he hung up the phone. I was thinking really hard where I know a Nisha from. No motherfucking way. It better not be my new client's hair who I've been doing. It sounded like her. If it was that bitch, she was getting fucked up. I paced my bedroom floor back and forth. My phone rang and it was Shawn. I answered the phone and played it off like I didn't hear his phone conversation. He was on his way home. I asked where he was coming from. He said he was coming from out South. Nisha stayed out South. We talked for a minute and ended the call.

Shawn and I had sex. Once I put his ass to sleep I went through his phone. I read text messages and forwarded the girl Nisha's number to my phone. His stupid ass doesn't even know how to cheat. You would think that he would erase the text messages out of his phone. I saw a few more numbers from other chicks. I forwarded as many numbers and messages as I could before Shawn woke up and caught me.

One Week Later...

Today, the girl Nisha had a hair appointment at 1 p.m. I also asked Shawn to bring me lunch around the same time. Nisha walked in about 12:37 p.m.

"Hey girl, what's up?" She said.

"Hello", I said being just as fake as her.

I finished my client hair by 1:10 p.m. Nisha got in my chair.

"How are you getting your hair today?" I asked as I wrapped the cape around her neck.

"Just a re-curl", she said.

I pulled out my phone and heated up the curlers. I called Nisha number private.

"Is that my phone ringing", she asked no one in particular.

I hung up and called it the phone again. Yes she was the Nisha that Shawn was fucking with.

"Nisha I'm going to ask you a question", I said.

"It's cool what's up?" She said.

"Are you fucking with a guy name Shawn?" She got quiet. That was a dead giveaway.

"No, I don't know any one named Shawn,"

Okay, so now this bitch was lying. From the conversation that I overheard on the phone she was aware that Shawn had a Wifey. Everyone in the beauty shop tuned in. I took the curlers out and burned that hoe across the side of her face.

"Hoe, don't play with me,"

She jumped up, "Bitch, is you crazy!"

"Yes hoe I am crazy, you got some balls coming in here to get your hair done by me and you fucking my man,"

"Bitch, fuck you!"

I jumped over my chair and smacked the fuck out of her. We were on the floor rumbling. Some of the clients tried their best to break us up and get me off of her. Shawn walked in the beauty shop. Nisha screamed for him to help her.

"Bitch shut the fuck up", I said.

The dumb hoe tried crawling away. I went after her but Shawn grabbed me.

"Put me down Shawn! Put me the fuck down", I screamed and kicked.

"Shawn help me, please. That bitch burned me!" Nisha cried.

I looked at Shawn.

"How could you?"

"Jas calm down. I didn't know that she was coming here to get her hair done,"

"But you're fucking the hoe. You fucking that hoe aren't you?"

Nisha left out the shop. Everyone ran outside to see where she was going. Shawn held me back and told me to stay inside. I ran behind him to see what all the commotion was about. Nisha got in her car. She hopped the curve and drove toward us. We ran and got out of the way. Nisha drove faster and another car came and crashed into her. Nisha's car spun around and slammed into a parked car. Everyone ran over to get her out of the car. I heard someone say that she was dead.

Chapter 6
Kelly

I hurried and rushed to the hospital. I didn't know what Shawn was talking about. All I heard was Jasmine, hospital, and police. When I got to the hospital I saw Shawn right away but I didn't see Jasmine.

"What's going on Brother? Where's Jasmine? Oh lord please don't tell me something happened to her,"

"Sis Jasmine is at the police station. She had a fight with this girl who she found out I was seeing on the side named Nisha. Nisha tried to run us over but another car ran into her and hit her,"
I'm looking at my Brother like who, what, when, where, and why?

"Shawn why are you up here and not at the police station with your woman?"

"Because I'm not going anywhere near a police station", Shawn said.

"Look I don't give a fuck about that girl in E.R. I'm sorry that it happened. But I'm getting out of here and going to see about my best friend Jasmine; if you're smart you should be following behind me!"

I left and went to the police station. Upon my arrival Ciara and Smooth was there.

"What's going on?" I asked.

"They are still questioning her. Where is Shawn?" asked Ciara.

"Let me talk to you in private,"

Ciara and I walked off to the side for some privacy. I filled her in on the story. She couldn't believe her ears either. Twenty minutes later Jasmine was released. Walking out the police station we saw Shawn sitting in his car. We all walked back to our cars. Jasmine got in the car with me. Ciara and Smooth went home. I pulled off, but Shawn cut me off.

"I'm sorry baby. Jasmine, baby what happened? What did they say?"

"Go to hell, Shawn. A girl is dead all because of you. You caused all of this. Then you have the nerve to act like you care and so concerned. You didn't give a fuck about me when you were fucking her,"

Shawn started to explain himself but Jasmine told me to drive off. We rode home in silence. I stayed with Jasmine overnight. I didn't feel comfortable leaving her alone. Shawn called her and she didn't answer. Jasmine gave me her phone. He started calling me and I told him that she doesn't want to be bothered. You have done enough just let her be.

The incident was all over the news. I turned the TV off, I didn't want to hear all the lies that the media told. I felt sorry for the girl Nisha's family. I was happy that Jasmine wasn't charged for anything.

Anthony called me.

"Hey baby. She's fine and resting now. I know it's all over the news, but I turned the TV off. I'm on the internet. What are you doing?"

Jasmine

Shawn kept on calling me. I was happy that Kelly had my phone. I really wanted to be alone right now. Thoughts of my parents flooded my head. I missed them so much and really wanted to be with them, I didn't mean for Nisha to die. I felt bad about that. I told the detectives that she started and initiated the fight. I wasn't going to tell them that I found out that she was sleeping with my man; and that's when I found out, so I beat her ass. Instead, I told them that she came into my shop and confronted me about sleeping with my man. We started arguing. She hit me and we fought.

Someone broke the fight up and she left the shop. Nisha jumped in her car and proceeded to drive into my shop. That's when another car hit her and she spun and hit a parked car. Never putting Shawn in the story and telling the detectives that he was there.

They asked who my boyfriend was; I gave them a fake name. They didn't have to know about him. I was pretty much done with him. After all this, I just wanted to die I went inside my purse and pulled out the bottle of Prozac. I took as many pills as I could and guzzled it down with the remaining Ciroc in my glass. I lay back down and drifted off to sleep.

Kelly

I and Anthony were engaged in a deep conversation about sex.

You so nasty Ant, I giggled.

"I love it when you do that thing with your tongue. Hold on Shawn is calling me again,"

"Hello", I said aggravated.

"She doesn't want to talk to you. She's in the room sleeping. Let me go and check on her,"

As I talked to Anthony on the phone I stopped paying attention to the internet. I walked in Jasmine room and I seen her lying across the bed in an uncomfortable position. Her mouth was twisted and her arm dangled from the bed.

"Jasmine, wake up", I shook her.

"Shawn something is wrong with Jas?"

I looked around the room and noticed an empty prescription bottle on the night stand.

"Shawn please come now, Jasmine took a bottle of pills. I don't know just how many, come now!"

I called 911; they told me check her pulse and asked if she was breathing. Her pulse was faint and breathing was shallow.

"OMG, please don't die on me Jasmine!"

They rushed Jasmine to the ER in the back. We were at Cook County Hospital. Shawn and I were the only people there for the time being. I tried my best to stay strong but I couldn't take seeing one of my best friends like that. The paramedics wouldn't tell us anything, but somehow I got a bad feeling. Everyone joined us at the hospital. It didn't take long for the doctor to come out and to tell us that they did the best that they could do. Jasmine was pronounced dead at 8:37 p.m.

The Funeral

As the young girl sang *"Amazing Grace"* I cried, my face was drenched with tears. Jasmine had a small private ceremony at Corbin's Funeral Home. Jasmine looked beautiful. She was dressed in all white and we had a crown on her head. It looked like she was sleeping. To make matters even worse, we found out at the hospital after her death that she was pregnant. The embryo had died as well. Everyone cried as the girl sang the song. Shawn was there, but we were separated; I was mad at my brother. I wished that my brother and my best friend hadn't got together now. Maybe she would still be alive. It was time for us to go around one more time before we headed to the burial. I approached Jasmine's coffin and said that I loved her and that she will always be my sister and best friend. I kissed her, Ciara joined me and we talked to Jasmine privately like she was still here. Everyone looked on and let us be and didn't interrupt us.

We buried her at Woodlawn Cemetery in Forest Park, Illinois. It was so hard seeing my friend go down in the ground. Ciara and I broke down. Everyone ran over to help us. We took it hard. We didn't want our best friend to leave us. I just couldn't believe this was really happening. Just the other day we were laughing, eating and joking. Damn I would give anything to have her back. She died so young. I wish I wasn't on the phone when she took them pills. I wish I could turn back the hands of time. They lowered her body down in the ground and Ciara and I threw our flowers to her. At the repast I didn't eat or talk to anyone. My grandma cooked the food and tried to get me to eat. I had no desire to even be here. I stepped outside on the back porch. Shawn joined me.

"Sis, I'm sorry for everything. I lost the love of my life over my stupid actions. If you hate me, I understand. If you want to beat me up, go ahead. If I could rewind everything, I would. I lost my sunshine and I don't want to lose my sister. I know it's going to take some time for you to for-give me. Whenever you ready to talk I will be ready,"

Shawn walked back inside the house and left me standing on the back porch. I stayed out there until the repast was over. Ciara came outside to join me and gave me a kiss and hug before she went home.

Chapter 7
Ciara

THREE MONTHS LATER…

"Happy Birthday to You, Happy Birthday to You, and Happy Birthday to Ciara" everyone sang.

Today was my 21st birthday. I was celebrating it with my family and friends; the people that I loved. I cried earlier because Jasmine wasn't here to share this moment with me. We rented out a hall and had food catered. We got a DJ and a photographer. The hall was beautifully decorated in my favorite color purple. I was having such a great time. I blew out all twenty-one candles on my triple layer birthday cake. It was time to open up my gifts. I sat in a chair on a stage and opened all my gifts and cards one by one. I felt so loved; I opened everyone's gift up except for Smooth's. He came on the stage and dropped down on one knee. I began to cry. I felt that moment was coming. He pulled out the box opened it up and the ring blinded me.

"Ciara, baby will you marry me?"

Everyone watched and waited for my response.

"Yes!"

Everyone cheered and clapped. I kissed Smooth long and hard. The photographer camera flashed as he took pictures. I was so happy and blessed. I danced with Smooth the entire night. For the first time I had a glass of wine. Everyone congratulated us on our engagement. It was getting late and I whispered something freaky in Smooth's ear. I was tipsy and was ready to lay down with my fiancée. The Moscato had me feeling some type of way. Smooth smiled and announced that it was time to wrap it up.

Rochelle

I sat back and watched Smooth and his "Wifey" got inside their car. It was Ciara's birthday and he had the nerve to throw her a party. He didn't even throw Erica a first birthday party or show up. His mother showed up and apologized for her son's absence. He sent a card with money inside it. He also had her gifts delivered. I was furious and wanted to fuck him up. I knew that as soon as "Wifey" had her baby, Smooth was going to forget about us. I overhead someone say Congrats. Congrats on what, I thought then I saw Ciara and two other girls admiring a ring on her finger. No the fuck he didn't propose to that bitch. Smooth know damn well he not ready to get married to anyone. They drove off and I followed them from a distance. Twenty minutes later he pulled up to a house in Westchester. Hmmm so he is buying houses too. I rode pass and waited to hit the block for the second time. I quickly wrote down their address. I hated the fact that Ciara had the family that I wished for. She had the house, the baby, and now the ring. I didn't stand a chance. Smooth didn't give a fuck about me. I was playing myself thinking that I still had a chance with him. I was in love with a man who didn't love me. I was going to let him forget about Baby Erica. "Wifey" you were going to get a surprised letter.

Three Days Later…

Ciara

I walked in the house with baby Eric on my hip. He was getting heavy. I kissed my baby on the forehead and sat him down on the couch. It was a crazy day and I was tired. My job still was not finished because I had to cook dinner. Damn, I wish I ordered take out instead. I went back to go pick the mail up from the floor. I had a manila envelope addressed to me along with some bills and magazines. I opened up the envelopes and it was a letter and a few pictures. My heart dropped as I looked at the pictures of Smooth, another woman, and a baby girl. The baby girl looked just like him. Oh my God, I was starting to feel lightheaded. I went over to sit next to Junior on the couch and read the letter.

Dear, Ciara

Hello you don't know me so I decided to reach out to you and introduce myself. My name is Rochelle and Smooth and I have been sleeping together. During our sex sessions a child was produced. I got pregnant and had a daughter by Smooth. Her name is Erica, yes she is named after Eric aka Smooth. She is one years old. Before you get to thinking if Erica is really his I have your answer. The DNA results are enclosed as well. I know you thinking why I am reaching out to you. I'm reaching out to you because I'm tired of him neglecting his daughter. I'm also tired of hiding my daughter like she is a secret. She has every right to be treated as his daughter too. I don't want to fight. I just want my daughter to be treated equally. Smooth didn't even show up for her 1 year old birthday party as a matter of fact he hasn't been involved in the last three months. He needs to get his act together before I seek legal action. Sorry that you had to find out this way.

Sincerely,

Rochelle

Two Hours Later…

Smooth walked in the house. I had put Eric Junior to bed. I was watching *Waiting to Exhale.*

"Hey baby", Smooth said. He kissed me, but I didn't kiss him back.

"We need to talk,"

He looked at me and said that he didn't feel like talking now.

"Oh yes the fuck you do. Explain this", I said, as I threw the letter and pictures at him.

"What is this?" He asked.

"You tell me. He looked at the pictures and had a dumb ass look on his face.

"Yes, you bastard, the secret is out!" I yelled. Tears were falling down my face.

"Ciara I'm sorry baby. I was going to tell you,"

SMACK! This time I smacked him.

"So this is the woman who has been calling your phone. This is the woman who you have been staying out late with. This is the woman whose scent you were wearing. This is the woman who scratched up my car. I just want to know how long you were going to hide this from me, Smooth. You were going to hide a child. Then you have the nerve to ask me to marry you. I don't even know who you are, you living double lives and shit. You fucking bitches raw; making babies with them. Here I am thinking that Junior was your first born. Not knowing that you at some other woman's house playing daddy,"

"I cheated on you once. We met, slept together and that was it. She called me and told me that I had a daughter. I was going to tell you, but I was afraid to lose you. I didn't mean to hurt you, Ciara baby. I cut her off and she got mad. That's the only reason why she mailed you all this. She wants us to separate. She's miserable and unhappy and she felt that having my baby would make me be with her. Baby, I swear that I love you. I just want to take care of my child, no strings attached. I know I was wrong for stepping out on you and creating a child, but she's here now and innocent. She doesn't deserve to be without a father,"

"Okay, you cheated and have a daughter. Smooth, I don't even know who you are. Who else knows?"

"My mother and of course I told my buddies", Smooth said.

"Look, right now I can't even think straight. I'm so mad that I could kill you. You got me looking stupid. I'm being loyal to you. You are the only man that I've ever loved and been with. You hurt me so many times that I've lost count. What you are going to do is take care of your daughter. She's a child and didn't ask to be here. She's more than welcomed into our home. You aren't allowed to go over to her house alone. If her mother wants to act pitiful and put the people in your business, that's your problem and not mine. I'm so tired of fighting with you. I'm tired of trying to make it work. Feel free to make yourself comfortable on the couch,"

Smooth was trying to apologize and make up. I didn't want to hear it. I was drained and hurt. I tuned him out. Right now I couldn't accept the fact that he had a child. I was cried out.
The next day I made a pop up visit at Rochelle's house. I rang the bell. She opened the door, but she didn't see me standing off to the side.

Pow! Pow! Pow! I hit that bitch in her mouth three times.

"What the fuck is going on?" She said in a daze.

"Bitch, you know what's up!" I said.

I beat that bitch ass. She didn't even fight back, dumb bitch. I didn't care; I was getting her back from fucking with my car and for sending me the letter. She was balled up in the corner of her porch. I eventually stop beating her ass. I walked away towards my car.

"Bitch this isn't over," Rochelle yelled.

"Hoe I ain't worried about you! Bring it bitch and if you keep on talking I'm coming back on that porch to finish beating your ass!" I said.

Her neighbors came outside looking at the confrontation. Rochelle ran back inside her house ashamed of what her neighbors had just witness. I jumped in my car and sped off.

Kelly

I was done with finals and passed all my classes. I don't know how I did it with everything going on around me. The lost of my best friend made me appreciate life. I took it hard and if it wasn't for Anthony, I would have lost it. At first I was upset with my brother Shawn, and blamed him for Jasmine's death. But after talking with my grandma, I decided to stop blaming him. I still wasn't talking to him until I was ready to talk without arguing. I go and visit Jasmine's grave site and to talk to her about me and Anthony. Yes, I'm still with him and not going anywhere. It's funny how close we have become. We are the talk of the west side. When you see him you see me. Shit that's my nigga. I still have to check a few hoes here and there, but they don't want any problems. I love the fact how Anthony and I keep these hoes mad. It's been peaceful since Ebony has been out of the picture. She still keeps my name in her mouth, but I don't pay her any attention. I just ignore the thirsty bitch. I'm not thinking about her ass. Anyway today I was joining my best friend Ciara at the spa. It was much needed and besides we had a lot of catching up to do.

At The Spa

"Are you telling me that Smooth has a one year old daughter? That's crazy. She was bold for mailing you a letter. You did exactly what I would've done and that was going to that bitch house to beat her ass. She didn't mail that letter to tell you about a baby, she mailed that letter to make you mad,"

"I felt the same way Kelly. At first she was fine hiding that fact that she had his child when he was spending time with her, the minute he stops putting in time, she wants to run her mouth. Ole stupid bitch. She thought she had him with that baby. But when Junior was born, I threw a monkey wrench in her dreams,"

"That bitch was dreaming. Her dumb ass had to wake up. How are you and Smooth? Are you still going to marry him?"

"Right now we together but separated. I made his ass move to the basement. I rarely say anything to him. I just need some space. I love him, but we have a lot to work on. Right now the wedding is off, but that could change in the future. I haven't told anyone about Smooth's other baby or about us not getting married. I just want it to work. I put so much time in this relationship that I don't want to walk away,"

"Ciara I understand whatever you choose to do is between Smooth and you. You don't have to worry about me telling anyone. I'm quite sure that Smooth is willing to do whatever he has to do to get his family back. If it takes today, tomorrow, next month, or next year so be it. I'm laughing at how you put Smooth's ass in the basement,"

We both started cracking up laughing. We finished up our spa day and I went back to her house to go spend time with my nephew. I realized I haven't spoken with Anthony since the earlier today. I called his phone several times and didn't get an answer. That wasn't like him. I went by his place and he wasn't there either. I stayed at his place just in case he decided to walk in the door with another bitch. The next day rolled around and Anthony didn't come home. I called his phone again but this time his voicemail popped on. I was getting worried. My phone rang and it was Anthony's mother calling me.

"Hello! No I haven't seen or spoken with him since earlier yesterday. I'm going to call Smooth and everyone right now,"

I called Smooth and they haven't seen or heard from him either. They had their people out in the streets looking for him. I was riding around looking for my man too, but I had no luck finding him. I had my phone attached to my heart just waiting for Anthony to call. Ciara told me to sit back and let the Fellas handle it. I decided to do that and chill at Ciara place. It was after 9 p.m. when I got the phone call from Vell.

"Hello what are you serious? Nooooo!"

After The Call

I was crying in Ciara arms not understanding what was going on. Anthony had been kidnapped and they wanted $30,000 to get him back alive. The money wasn't a problem. I just wanted to know who was behind this kidnapping. I pray that they don't kill him. Vell said the caller wanted the money in twenty-four hours or else he was dead. They spoke to Anthony just to make sure that he was still alive. One of Smooth's workers found Anthony truck abandoned on the south side. It was off to the side of the road and looked as though they pulled him out of it. It was clean and they couldn't find any evidence in it to help them. Anthony's mother was going crazy. I just wished it was all a nightmare and I woke up and everything was back to normal.

Ciara tried her best to comfort me. I was speechless for the first time. I just wanted to be alone right now. I couldn't lose Anthony. Bad enough I had just lost my best friend four months ago. I fell asleep in Ciara's extra bedroom. Smooth and everyone felt like it was best to keep an eye on me. Hours later I was awaken by Smooth and

Ciara arguing. Listening to them wasn't easy. Shifting in a comfortable position I faced the wall just staring at it. All I could think about was Anthony; praying that my man was alive. Craving to be in his arms right now and laying on his chest. A thousand things went off in my head as I thought of all the bad things that they could be doing to him.

Today I decided that I wasn't going to cry. I was going off to find my man. My ringing phone snapped me back into reality. I jumped and answered quickly when I noticed Anthony number pop on to my screen.

"Hello", I said. No one answered but instead I heard talking on the other end of the phone. I listened and heard a familiar voice. Listening closely for any details that the kidnappers would drop, I had my phone glued to my ear. Three minutes later the call ended. I walked into the bedroom that Ciara and Smooth shared and said, "I'm going to kill that Bitch!"

"Who?" asked Ciara.

"Ebony, she has Anthony!"

Chapter 8
Smooth

Damn finding out that Ebony's hoe ass was behind Anthony's kidnapping wasn't surprising to me. That money hungry hoe got her money any way she could. We always told Anthony to watch out for that dirty hoe. I called up everyone to tell them the news. Kelly begged to ride out with us, but I couldn't let her go. I understand how bad she wanted a piece of Ebony, but right now it wasn't about her. We had to get my man back alive. We got the phone call to drop the bag of money off at an abandoned warehouse in the south suburbs. I had my shooters armed and ready. The place was dark inside. We scoped out the area and it wasn't a person in sight. We dropped the bag of at the spot where the kidnappers told us. We got a call and they told us we were good to go.

"Fuck that, where's Anthony?" I said.

"Be cool nigga we gonna give you back your man", the caller then laughed on the other end of the line.

We left the warehouse, but we had three of our shooters hiding in the cut waiting for the niggas to pick up the money. Twenty minutes later a black van pulled up and three masked man jumped out. One grabbed the money while the other two watched his back. He opened up the bag to check to see if all the money was there. The other men pulled Anthony out of the van. He was blindfolded and his hands were tied behind his back. One of the masked men put the barrel of the gun against the back of Anthony head, but he was eliminated by one of my shooters. The other two masked men looked around and started firing. They couldn't fuck with my shooters. They were trained killers. They aired their asses out in one minute. When the coast was clear we moved in to grab Ant.

"Be cool nigga it's me Vell,"

Ant was untied and the blindfolded taken off. We placed him in the car and grabbed the bag of money. Before we left we pulled off the mask of the three men. One of them was Rich and two of his Niggas. Before I left, I popped one of them slugs in Rich forehead.

A week passed and we were still looking for Ebony. We went by her father's house, but the old man wasn't talking and we put one in his head. We put a bounty on Ebony's head for twenty-five thousand dollars. Word spread fast around the city and everyone wanted a piece of that action. We knew Ebony couldn't get far; she was on the run with a newborn baby. Shunda, Rich's baby mama informed us that she had family in Dallas, and could be on the way there. I called my cousin Tommy, and he and his people were on it.

Ebony

Shit went all wrong. I realized after three hours had past that Rich didn't make it. The news came on in the morning and confirmed my suspensions.

"Breaking news, we're live at an abandoned warehouse located in South Holland, Illinois; where African-American males were found dead. All three had been shot multiple times. A black van and masks were also discovered at the scene of the crime. So far we have no suspect or suspects in custody and we don't have the identity of the victims. Reporting live I'm Damara White from ABC 7 News,"

I gathered up all of my things and got out of the house as fast as I could. Me and baby Kimora got out of there. Knowing sooner than later that they would come looking for me. I had enough cash put away. Rich and I had been setting up niggas for the last two months. Rich approached me about the idea because he was fucked up. Due to him being my baby father I was obligated to help him get back on. It was easy setting up niggas. I made an IG page and posted up sexy pictures of myself to get the niggas attention. It didn't take long for they thirsty ass to come flocking. Most of the people following me were from Chicago. They stunted so hard on the social site. Posting pictures of their money, cars, and jewelry. They would post and comment on my pictures to holler at me. I only exchanged numbers with few we knew were caked up. I got up with one another and we fucked. It was easy getting information out of them because they kept me around. Whenever they called asking for this pussy, I was available.

It was amazing what pussy will do. By the time we rob them, they wouldn't see it coming. Sometimes I was there on the scene and got hurt and played like I didn't know what was going on. The shit was easy and I would just move on to the next nigga. One day Rich came in and suggest that we hit Anthony. I told him that it would be hard to get him. I called Anthony up but he wasn't on shit with me. He was too in love with that bitch Kelly. That shit made me mad. Rich was getting frustrated and that's when they came up with idea that they would kidnap him. I didn't give a fuck I never loved him. I sped down the express way real fast. I was nervous as fuck. I wasn't trying to get caught up in that bullshit. I wasn't worried about the authorities. I was worried about my life.

It's been four hours since I've been on the road. I pulled over at a cheap motel. Kimora needed to be cleaned and I needed to get some rest. My phone rang the entire time from family members, I didn't answer. I called one of my male cousins back and he told me that my father had been killed and that they had a bounty on my head. I know Smooth and them didn't play any games. Fuck, how did I get involved in this bullshit? My cousin asked where I was headed, but I didn't tell him. In the morning I got baby Kimora cleaned up and we hit the road again. I had nine more hours to go before I got to Dallas.

Five Months Later...
Kayla

I was looking at a new place today. My lease was up next month and I was ready to move and find a bigger place. I picked out another place in Lombard, Illinois. It was nice and I was happy that the landlord accepted Section 8. Smooth was paying me more. I was able to buy me new furniture for every room in the house. I also had more responsibilities. Now I was dropping off and picking up. I still held the safe and drugs inside my place for Smooth. We fucked, but not as much as we used to. He and Ciara had problems that they were going through, so I decided to fall back until he wanted me. I also go a new car and was now pushing a Volkswagen truck. I was happy that I was growing up. I stop clubbing and start sitting back. I filled out the application for the apartment and the man said that he would give me a call in two days. I headed out, we had a meeting today and I had to be there on time. When I got there everyone was there. Vell was talking about our moves that we were making down in Dallas. They planned on flying down there and taking care of business next month. I wanted to go so bad. I haven't been out of Chicago and now I could finally afford it. I had to try to get Smooth to take me. Smooth came over to visit me. I was happy now it was time for me to work my magic on him. I cooked up some food and fed him. Once we were done I fucked him and he busts a huge nut down my throat.

"Damn Kayla that head still fye", he said.

I swallowed up the nut and said, "Yes, daddy you deserve the best,"

It was time for me to bring up Dallas.

"Baby, can I go to Dallas with you and the crew? I've never been out of Chicago and you never take me anywhere,"

"Kayla I don't know. I was taking Ciara with me. If I wasn't, you could have come, but I don't think it would be a good idea to have you and her down there at the same time. I don't want y'all to bump heads. Ciara and I are finally getting back along.

I was mad, but I understood what he was saying. I had to make my money and I didn't need any altercation with Ciara. Smooth explained to me that if I was going to be messy, that he was going to cut me off. I didn't want to go back to living average and just depending on my SSI check. So I followed all the rules and stayed the fuck out of Ciara's way and I played my role. Smooth got up and left and threw me a few dollars.

"Don't worry beautiful, I will take you out of town real soon", he said.

I just said okay and locked the door behind him. Walking in the bathroom I turned the shower on and it sounded like I heard Smooth cursing someone out. I headed to look out the window and he was arguing with a dark skinned girl who had a little girl with her. The little girl looked just like Smooth. It had to be his other baby momma I heard about Rochelle, and his daughter, Erica. The little girl was beautiful. Smooth bent down to kiss and hug her, but the girl pulled her away from him. I stayed inside and watched everything from outside my window. The little girl cried for Smooth. I just shook my head and I couldn't wait to move first; Ciara comes to my house trying to fight me and now this bitch Rochelle was popping up here too. Smooth pushed Rochelle and told her to get the fuck on. She left leaving him there with his daughter. Smooth walked back towards my door and I let him in.

"Kayla, this is my daughter Erica I need you to watch her for a few hours while I go handle this business,"

I said sure. Once he left I turned on cartoons and Erica sat down to watch them.

Ciara

Smooth and I had been doing fine and working on our relationship. We had to meet with the wedding planner. I was already at her office waiting on Smooth to arrive. He came and was fifteen minutes late. I didn't even have time to get mad. I was just happy that he showed up. We went over everything and decided on the location, colors, and the food. I was so happy that I hired a wedding planner. All this stuff was too much for me to handle. The wedding planner's name was Nicole and she was very pleasant and nice. She was happy that we were getting married and planning traditional services. She was black and I loved supporting my own people. We left and she said she would keep in touch with us. Nicole was very professional and I liked that about her. I said my goodbyes and told her I was looking forward to her services.

Once we got outside the place, Smooth went on to explain why he was late. I stopped him from talking and instead kissed him on the lips. I didn't even want to hear it and I didn't even care. He's never on time and that's okay with me as long as he made it. I hugged him and told him I would see him tonight when I got home. On my way back to the boutique I was thinking about the first day I met him and how far we have came. We've been through so much. Losing Jasmine and the kidnapping of Anthony made me realize that I didn't want to lose him. We both decided to work on everything to get our family back in together.

It was busy at the Bella Boutique. London was still my assistant but she was branching off to open up her own shoe store soon. I was so happy for her. When people come to shop with me once they were done, I could send them to her to get their shoes. We have to support one another. We were busy picking and selecting shoes out that I didn't even notice Rochelle walk in. My day was going pleasant and I didn't have time for her bullshit. Why the fuck was she up here anyway.

"Excuse me why are you here? Every time I look up I see you. Do I have to get a restraining order against you? I guess you haven't learned from the last ass whopping that I gave you,"

"Silly bitch I came up here to tell you about your soon to be husband leaving another bitch's house. Oops, did I just say that. Oh, I believe I did. So you might want to look into that,"

Rochelle turned to walk out of the boutique. I didn't pay her any mind; I know that Smooth and I had just left from seeing the wedding planner. I continued on running my business, but I was thinking in the back of my mind is that why Smooth was running late. I hurried home and was surprised that Smooth was already there.

"Your crazy-ass baby mother still stalking me and shit, Rochelle came up to the shop today and said that you were leaving another woman's house. What is she talking about Smooth? You know you can't do anything with her or in front of her without her coming to throw the shit back in my face,"

"I don't know what her crazy ass talking about. I ran into her earlier before we had to meet the wedding planner. She was talking shit like she usually does. Don't pay Rochelle any attention baby. I'm gonna check her ass about coming up to your boutique,"

Smooth hugged me from behind.

"Yeah ok", I said.

Part of me felt that Rochelle wasn't lying on Smooth. She was a woman scorned and she would do anything to separate us. Rochelle hated the fact that we were still getting married, after I found out about her daughter. When she seen that the baby didn't work she tried several things to destroy us. She was getting on my fucking nerves. I was tired of beating her ass because she can't fight. Maybe I should get a restraining order against her. My mother, Smooth's mother, and London thought that as well.

The next day before I went to open up the boutique, I stopped by the police station to put a restraining order against Rochelle. I was protecting myself and I wasn't scared of her. I got it just in case she came for me I could fuck her up without being charged. The lady is crazy she already tried several attempts to get me locked up. And to be honest I don't need a background. I filled out the paperwork. After I was done I was on my way to the boutique, Kelly called me and we were on the phone talking. During our conversation I could have sworn someone was following me. I told Kelly that I would call her back. I turned right and the Volkswagen turned right. I continued to drive down Chicago Avenue; she was still behind me. I wasn't too far from the boutique.

Five minutes later, I whipped in a park in front of the boutique. The Volkswagen rode past and the female in the car laughed as she rode by. It was that bitch, Kayla. I see she got herself a new car. That little bitch Kayla think I forget about her. I was just playing it cool. I was just playing it cool. I've been aware of her since last year when I went by the slow hoe house. Apparently, she was holding his shit and if the bitch wanted to, so be it. She just better be ready to do the time, if the people come running in there. Deep down inside I felt that Kayla and Smooth were still fucking. I wasn't going to stop fucking with Smooth so these hoes can have him. To be honest, Smooth didn't want to stop fucking with me. How cute is her little Volkswagen I chuckled. My thoughts were interrupted by Smooth's phone call.

"Hello, I just pulled up in front of the boutique. Your girlfriend Kayla just followed me all the way to work. Yes, I guess she wanted me to see her new Volkswagen. You know that's your girlfriend, she lucky I'm in a good mood. I'm tired of your hoes fucking with me. Anyway kiss Junior for me and tell him that Mommy loves him. No I don't love you", I laughed.

"You better love me, you don't have a choice", I said laughing.

"Love you too goodbye,"

Today was going to be a good day. I didn't have time for the bullshit.

Chapter 9
Rochelle

Closing the door behind the officer I went to sit down on my sectional. Ciara had put a restraining order against me. I laughed and picked up my phone to call Smooth.

"Hello, so Wifey want to put the police in it. I didn't call the police when she came to my house and beat my ass. I took that ass whopping and kept it moving. Tell you about those want to be tough bitches." I laughed into the phone.

"Rochelle you need to grow up. Why are you calling Smooth's phone with this bullshit?! Yes it's me Ciara are you surprised? And hoe, I never thought I was tough, but I know one thing I'm far from scared. You don't have shit else better to do than to stalk me. I'm afraid if I didn't know any better I would think that you were infatuated with me." Ciara said laughing.

"Bitch please don't flatter yourself. You aren't all that boo, but your man dick is. That's why I'm going to forever stay sucking and fucking it. Whether you put a restraining order against me or not, it's not going to stop that. I'm his baby's momma, bitch you have to deal with me forever.

Ha Ha Ha. I'm not going anywhere. Bitch when you look up I'm gonna always be there." I said.

"Funny, I'm the one with the ring. Its four carats and really nice, where's your ring?" Ciara asked laughing.

I got quiet and choked up a little bit.

"You crazy, don't any men want you. Hell, you a nurse and can't even get a doctor. Yes, I heard about how you thought it was his baby. Ha Ha Ha. Who's laughing now? My man tells me everything, so why you busy sucking and fucking him, please remember that when you're done he's right back here with me. Matter of fact, I'm laying on his chest now. Say Hi to your baby momma."

"What's up?" Smooth said laughing into the phone.

I hung up the phone. I was hurt and pissed at how Smooth has taken her side. This nigga was just fucking me and now he saying fuck me. I hate that little young bitch Ciara! He got the fucking nerves to buy her a ring. Four carats at that. I was so upset that he was discussing me with that bitch. How could he tell her my personal information like that!? I felt betrayed and like I was fucking a stranger. Most of all it finally hit me in the face that Smooth no longer cared about me. I had plans on becoming his chick and kicking Ciara to the side. Smooth had no right to cut me off. I went in my bedroom and start throwing darts at Smooth's picture that I had on the wall. I fucking hated him. I picked up my phone and called him again.

"Hello." Ciara said into the phone.
"Bitch put Smooth on the phone! Why in the fuck are you answering his phone anyway?!" I said.
"Because I'm his woman and I can answer his phone. What do you want Rochelle?! You don't have another man to stalk?" Ciara said.
"I keep forgetting that you're young and naïve. I don't have time to be playing on the phone with your dumb ass! Put Smooth on the phone!" I yelled

It got quiet for a minute. For a second I thought she hung up the phone. I could hear their child in the background crying. My heart sank when I heard Smooth talk to his baby boy and say Daddy's here. I listened so more and realized that Ciara had put the phone down on purpose just so I can hear their conversation. I hung up and called them right back. Smooth answered the phone.

"What Rochelle!?" Smooth said.

"Why Smooth? Why are you treating me this way? What about our daughter? It's not fair Smooth. Then you got the nerve to be buying that lame bitch a ring." I said.

"Rochelle look, Ciara is my woman and you need to respect that. I don't have time to be playing games with your silly ass. What is my daughter doing?" Smooth said.

"She's sick." I lied and said.

"What's wrong with her?" Smooth asked.

I stuttered and didn't really know what to say. You would think that me becoming a nurse and all that I could come up with something. I decided to say that she had a fever.

"She has a fever." I said.

"Did you give her something for the fever?" Smooth asked.

I could hear Ciara in the background talking. She snatched the phone away from Smooth.

"Look bitch ain't shit wrong with your daughter so please stop lying. You're trying really hard to get Smooth over there. What you failed to realize is that when Smooth move, I move. Meaning that I will be right by his side when it comes to seeing his daughter." Ciara said.

"Little girl you sound crazy if you think when Smooth come by to visit his daughter that you are welcomed as well. You really sound crazy." I said.

"You know what Rochelle I'm getting tired of you calling me a little girl. When the only person who not acting their age right now is you. Aren't you a nurse? Shouldn't a fever be simple for you to treat? I'm going to be the adult that I am right now and end this call. I have something that you don't have that's a family and I'm not going to allow you to break that up. HaHaHa you a lonely bitch." Ciara said ending the call.

"Click!"

We will see who gets the last laugh when I'm done!

Kayla

Smooth called me last week telling me he was gonna fuck me up if I followed Ciara again. I was pretending as though I didn't know what he was talking about. After he tried to check me, I ran the water for my bath. Today was a busy day for me. Earlier I packed as much as I could prepare to leave next month. Plus, I went to pick up some more coke to put together and I had to drop it off. I didn't feel like going to drop it off and wanted to wait until tomorrow. But I got my lazy ass up and went to handle my business. Now I was I was back home. It was a long day for me. I smelled and needed to get my stinky ass in the tub.

Relaxing in the water I thought about how much Smooth and I have been through. We fight, we talk, we argue, we text, we smile, we laugh, and we love. That's us. That nigga was crazy if he thought I cared about Ciara feelings. Fuck her; he doesn't even care about her because if he did, he and I wouldn't be still fucking. I came before the bitch anyway but I still finished last. That shit is crazy, she got the ring and the house and I'm still where I started. Sometimes I feel emotional about it. It was only right that I had a certain amount of jealousy inside of me when it came to her. Fuck love. This time I was only thinking about me and only me. I was putting my heart to the side. My focus was only going to be on getting money; nothing else but money. A motherfucker has never loved me.

I got out the water and applied baby oil to my body. Wrapped my hair up and turned on the TV. I watched the news and it was the same old shit just a different day; shootings, killings, mothers crying over losing their child, and mug shots across the screens of young black males. Chicago was grimy. It's not even safe to sit in your house. So when you hit the streets you better be strapped. You better believe I keep it on me. Watching the news was depressing so I made it a Netflix night.

I was laughing so hard at Kevin Hart silly ass that I didn't even here them coming.

BOOM! The FBI kicked down my door and came rushing in on me.

"What the fuck is going on?" I asked.

Twenty FBI agents came running inside the house.

"Freeze!"

They drew their guns, cuffed me, and flashed their badges. They showed the search warrant and they had a picture of me. I watched many agents throw my shit around and break things. They were in every room. The even looked in the damn refrigerator. They were in my bedroom and I couldn't see what was going on. I had Smooth guns in my closet. Now I wished like hell that I wasn't holding them. I have section 8 and that's a violation to have firearms in my home. I wanted to cry but I didn't. I felt that if anything happened that Smooth would come and save me. All I heard was noise coming from out of the room. I wonder who in the fuck called them. No one knew where I stayed. It was liked they had a tip or something. I sat there quietly as one of the agents asked me questions. I wasn't saying shit. I'm not no fucking snitch.

"Get dressed!" One of the agents yelled.

They took my ass outside and threw me in the back of the police car. It was seven cars and a van outside. I watched as they went through my house and tearing shit up. Lucky for me that I dropped the drugs off earlier.

"Fuck!" I said under my breath.

I had guns and money inside the house. I was going to be fucked when they found it. The car drove off and took me to the station.

I was in the room sitting in hand cuffs as one of the agents interrogated me. I didn't say a word. He tried to get me to talk several times and threaten me on many occasions. He told me that they found dope in my house. I knew that was a fucking lie because I had got rid of it earlier. I didn't fall for that trick. Ten minutes later another agent walked inside the room and told me that they found the guns.

"Kayla I know the guns aren't yours. Whose guns are you holding?" The agent asked.

"I don't know what you're talking about." I said.

"Look we could make this easy for you. Why don't you tell us where did the guns come from. We will make sure that you walk out of here and only get probation." The agent said.

"Can I please make a phone call?" I asked irritated.

"Who you gonna call, your boyfriend? He can't save you because our buddies is at his place right now." The agent said.

My heart dropped and start pacing fast. Get it together Kayla, don't let them see you sweet. I said in my head. I hope that they don't have Smooth. I need him to help me out and if he gets grabbed then I'm fucked.

Rochelle

Sitting in my car I watched from a distance as the FBI agents were going back in forth inside Smooth's and Ciara's home. Moments later they bought Smooth out the house in handcuffs. He had on a wife beater and some jogging pants. I waited to see if they were going to bring Ciara out, but they never did. Everyone came outside their homes to see what was going on. The entire street was blocked off. It was at least ten cars outside. Ciara neighbors watched from their porches. Damn, I thought they were never going to finish. It took them hours to search their home and finally they were done. They left with a few things. Damn, why didn't they lock her up? Ciara slammed her front door with Junior in her arms. I drove off laughing. That's what the bitch gets for fucking with me. I dropped the dime on her and Smooth three months ago. I called them about Smooth, Ciara, and his side bitch Kayla.

I didn't give a fuck about Kayla. But since she was fucking with Smooth, that bitch had to go down with them too. Of course in the process of watching Smooth, along came Vell, Ant, and Red. I didn't mean for all them to go down but shit happens so fuck it. It was only noon and it was all over town. I hope Smooth goes to jail for a very long time. I was mad that they didn't take Ciara into custody. I was hoping that she lost everything; her house, car, and all her designer clothes and had to start all over again. I was hoping that DCFS came in and took Junior away from her. It was still early so, hopefully, one of them talks and they come back to get Ciara to charge her with something. Damn, they didn't hit her boutique. I told them about that as well. That's ok, I would handle that. Ciara is going to wish that she didn't fuck with me and when this was all over I was going to get the last laugh.

Ciara

I cried as I walked through my house. The FBI came in here and tore up everything. They ripped up my couch, destroyed my clothes, and went through my fridge. Food was everywhere. It was a mess. Junior's room was a disaster. And I don't even want to tell you what my basement looked like. My mother and Kelly were there to help me out. They had Smooth in custody, but they didn't find shit inside the house. I was waiting to hear back from his lawyer. The Feds also came in my boutique, but it was nothing in there either. We took our time and cleaned up everything. I was so embarrassed my neighbors seen everything, but they were very supportive and asked if I needed any help. I had to replace the back door. They came in through the back at 6 a.m. in the morning.

"FBI, FBI, FBI, Get your arms up and don't you move them! Walk downstairs right now. Do not move your hands!"

I watched as they disrespected Smooth and dragged him out the house. I held on tight to Junior. They ushered me and my baby to the couch, and then proceeded to search my house. Junior cried because of all the chaos that was going on. I did my best to calm my baby down. They asked me about me about my boutique, but I ignored them and didn't say anything. My home was ransacked and I was shaken up. They found nothing, or had anything that they could charge him with. Smooth never kept shit where he laid his head.

According to the search warrant they were looking for illegal weapons and drugs it took the agents three hours to search my house. By that time Junior was sleeping in my arms. When they left I locked the front door and called Smooth's mother's, my mother, and Kelly. They all got to me as fast as they could. I learned from Kelly that everyone else was in custody too. Ms. Robinson took Junior back to her house to keep him. Hours later, I finally heard back from Smooth's lawyer and he said that they were going to release him, but he didn't know how soon it would be. They didn't come up with a reason to keep him or the others, but they were giving them a hard time questioning him about the house, cars, and the material possessions.

He also told me that the Feds received a call from someone stating that we had drugs and guns inside the house and that Smooth was a big time drug dealer. I don't know who and it could've been anyone in the streets of Chicago. I thanked him and got off the phone with him to continue to clean up my home. My mother and Kelly were a big help. I was too nervous to sleep there overnight by myself. They both stayed over and ordered a pizza since I didn't have any food to eat inside the house. I couldn't eat anything. I was waiting to hear from Smooth. My mother told me not to worry and to get some rest. At 1 a.m. I received a phone call. I answered the phone in hopes that it was Smooth. Instead it was someone from the fire department telling me that my boutique was on fire.

Chapter 10

Kelly

Three Months Later…

Anthony and I were like two love birds. After the incident we both found a place and decided to move together. We grew closer to one another. I was still going to school to pursue my career and he was still in the streets getting that bread. I woke up from a long night of lovemaking. Stretching my body from a long night, my arms went flying in the air and came back down. That's when I seen it.

"Oh my God, Oh my God, are you serious?" I screamed in joy.

While I was sleeping, Anthony had placed a ring on my finger. I was staring at the ring and it was nice. Anthony came walking in the room smiling.

"I see you finally woke up", he said.

"Oh baby its beautiful", I said while jumping in his arms.

"So that means that you will marry me?" He asked.

"Yes baby, I will marry you,"

I started to kiss him, but he stopped me and said, "Morning Breath!"

We started laughing so hard.

I called everyone and shared the news; Ciara was so happy for me, and Junior even clapped his hands for his Auntie Kelly. I called my grandma and she already knew about it. She said Anthony called and asked for her permission. She also told me that I should talk to my brother Shawn. I promised my grandma that I would call him. Later on that day my mother called me collect and I shared the news with her as well. She was happy that I found the love of my life. I told her that I couldn't wait t see her and she also told me to call my brother. Finally after everyone told me to call my brother, I pushed my pride to the side and called him. The phone rang several times, but he didn't answer. Oh well, I called him. Maybe he is busy. Shawn was in California. After losing Jasmine he felt like he needed a change of scenery. Jumping out of the bed I went in the closet to pick out something to wear for tonight. Anthony was taking me out for dinner and I wanted to be sexy. I choose an all white Christian Dior dress with my white sling backs. I was happy that I was finally celebrating something. The last couple of months were crazy with all the shootings, killings, kidnapping, and federal cases. Chicago was wild, but I loved my city. Sometimes I just wish that

Anthony and I could go somewhere far away from here.

We had dinner at Grand Lux. I made sure I ordered chocolate chip cookies to go. Their cookies were the bomb. As soon as we got home I stripped down to nothing. I went inside the kitchen to get the whip cream. I put whip cream on my nipples and my pussy. Love making was the only thing on my mind. I lie down and spread my legs wide open. Anthony came in and gently placed his tongue on my nipples. I loved when he sucked my titties he took his time one by one. Slowly working his way down my licking my stomach; his tongue felt amazing. His tongue circled my belly button and working his way downtown. He stopped and focused on my inner thighs. Damn, he knew that was my hotspot. My clit jumped for attention. Ant flicked it with his tongue giving me a tease. He ate my pussy like it was his last meal. Legs in the air, his face buried deep as his tongue performed magic. Doing tricks that I didn't know exist. Running from his tongue, I wasn't ready to let my juices flow. His tongue was winning first place.

"Oh Oh, I'm about to cum,"

Legs shaking in the air, he sucked up all my juices; exhaling all my worries away.

Rochelle

I was out in the clubs partying like I used to do before I had Erica. We were at Hearts a popular night club. I was with three of my other girlfriends. It was a Monday night and we were out popping Mollies and Bottles. I experimented with drugs quite a few times but nothing never really major to get me hooked. I love doing extacy because it made the sex better. One of my friends asked me if I ever fucked a guy while he was off a Molly and I never had before. She said that it was the best. So tonight I was trying to find out. Hearts was jumping and it was a lot of money in the building. Me and my girlfriends dance on one another to get the men's attention. We had our own VIP section. Don't get it wrong we made good money, but we were also into spending other people money too.

My friend Porsha was so happy that I was back partying with them. I was still young, twenty-four years old and even though I had a baby, I still had it. We had been drinking everything from Ciroc to Patron; I had to go to the bathroom. As I walked through the crowd men grabbed my hand to get my attention. I rushed inside the bathroom and cut all those bitches in line. I heard a girl say something, but I didn't give a fuck I had to piss and Rochelle wasn't waiting in a line for nothing. When I got out the stall the girl looked like she wanted to say something and I dared her too. I washed my hands and left out. When I made it back to our section my friends was talking to some guys. I sized them up and I picked which one I wanted.

We conversed a bit and after the party was over we all went out to breakfast and I ended up at his place. His name was Toby and he stayed over east in a condo. We had sex in the shower and we made it to the bed. Toby dick was average but he knew how to work it. He fucked me from behind while choking, spanking, and pulling my hair. OMG, it felt good to finally be fucking someone else other than Smooth. He pumped rapidly into my pussy and I got wetter. That's right Toby hit that pussy, just like that I said. He hit my pussy from the back until I exploded.

The next day I got up and left to go home. Toby wanted me to stay a little longer, but I had to leave to get home to my daughter. I promised him that I would give him a call. I was lying I wasn't going to call him again. I got home and paid the babysitter and spent the rest of the day with my daughter. Friday night came and I and my girls were partying again. This time we went to KOD the strip club. We had our own VIP section again and bottle after bottle. I popped a Molly and I was feeling myself. Everyone was in there; it was the place to be. I got a lap dance from a stripper called Lollipop. She was caramel, thick and maybe 5'5" with a big ass. She popped her pussy for me like I was a nigga, I didn't do girls but tonight I was willing to give it try. I and my girlfriends took pictures and we were having a good time. We had a ball and I made it rain on Lollipop when she hit the stage. Before I left we exchanged numbers. By the end of the night I was in Lollipop's bed getting my pussy ate. Her tongue felt amazing and she made me squirt. Damn, I came four times with this bitch. My first girl on girl experience was amazing. In the morning I got up and had to leave. I kissed Lollipop goodbye and promised to call her tomorrow. I wasn't lying to her; she was definitely getting a call back.

I was right back to being a party girl and found myself going out at least three days out of the week. I would meet different niggas, and they would want to take me out to eat, take me shopping, some wanted to trick off while others wanted relationships. I was just taking advantage of it all. Hell, Smooth didn't want to be with me. No more trying to settle down with one man. I was back to the old Rochelle; only this time I'm not getting pregnant. I stop letting Smooth see Erica. I changed my number on him. I got tired of him calling me. He can sign his rights away and that would be fine with me.

I was getting ready to go out on a night with this new nigga that I had met three days ago. My friend Porsha called me and asked if I wanted to go out to Club Bodi tonight. I told her that I would meet her up there after my date. I had a babysitter; why not stay the night out.

It was a Sunday night and I was at Club Bodi partying with my bestie Porsha. We stayed in the crowd and we mingle and met different men. We drank and snapped up a lot of pics with different people. The Chicago Bears was up in the party. One of them sent us a bottle each of Moet and asked us both to go back with him at the hotel. I asked him what he was paying. He said $2,500 a piece; I and Porsha was down, that was half of my mortgage. We partied some more and I popped a Molly. It made me feel good and relaxed. Once the party was over we met up with him at the hotel. The threesome started off with both me and Porsha sucking his dick. He told Porsha to sit on his face while I continued to suck his dick. He fucked Porsha from behind as she ate my pussy. He pulled out of her and starting fucking me, and Porsha still licked on my clit. I sucked on her breast and told her to hop on my face. She rode my face as he fucked the shit out of me. We fucked all night long.

The next afternoon I woke up and my phone was dead we got our money and Porsha and I left. As soon as I got in my car I plugged my charger in my phone. My alerts went off on my phone. I called my babysitter and she sounded so hysterical and told me that Erica's father had come by the house to get her. She said that she had been calling me all morning trying to reach me and that she didn't want to call the police because Smooth threatened her. I was pissed and hung up the phone. I jumped on the west suburbs ramp and was on my way to go get my baby.

I pulled up in front of Smooth's house and jumped out of my car, I wasn't even parked but I didn't give a fuck. I banged on his door and Ciara answered.

"Bitch why the fuck you banging on my door?" Smooth jumped in front of her.

"Give me back my daughter. You have no right to take my baby", I yelled.

"Rochelle get your ass off my porch. You think you can just take my daughter from me? I have rights too. Go home and sober up because right now you look a mess. I see you back partying again; someone texted me some pictures. I don't know why you out here like that,"

"I can do whatever the fuck I want to as long as I take care of my child. Smooth, just give me my daughter!"

He went inside and closed the door on me. I banged on the door, but they didn't answer. I went to pick up one of the flower pots out the yard and busted out the front window. Ciara came outside and beat my ass. I thought she was gonna kill me. The police came and I went running to them and told him that he took my daughter. The police wasn't trying to hear me and they arrested me for destruction of property and for breaking the restraining order that Ciara had against me. I was handcuffed and taken to jail. Before I was put inside the police car I told Smooth this shit isn't over.

Ebony

I was down in Dallas living low-key with my baby girl Kimora. I had a few family members down here but I wasn't letting know that I was nearby. I stayed in a small one bedroom; I had fifty thousand to live off of. I bought a little used car for five thousand. I stayed inside most of the time; only going out to get groceries or the things that I needed. When I went out I stayed to myself and took Kimora with me everywhere. Being on the run wasn't any fun. I wanted to go out and party, meet new niggas, and most of all go out and fuck. I haven't had any dick in a long time. You know how I love to fuck and besides Kimora needed a step daddy. I really miss her father Rich. When I finally got him to myself, he was taken away. I remember when we first started creeping around behind my best friend's Shunda back. It was the summer of 2011, yes, three years ago.

After Rich's Annual Barbecue that he had every summer at Garfield Park. Me and my best friend Shunda was excited about going. All the hating hoes from out west were going to be there. We were both dressed nice for a barbecue. Shunda had on a one piece short abstract print romper with a pair of wedges. I had on two piece white short set with my white wedges on. As soon as we got there all eyes were on us. We partied until the police came and broke it up at 1 a.m. We jumped in the van and didn't want to go home, so we went to the lakefront. Everyone knows how we kick it at the lakefront in Chicago. We kicked it down there drinking and smoking. I walked backed to the van to get my cell phone and stayed inside the van for privacy. Ten minutes later Rich came back to the van to grab a bottle of Patron.

"Damn girl, I didn't know you were in here. Next time you better say something girl. You almost got shot", Rich said.

I got off the phone and laughed at Rich.

"I'm sorry; I thought y'all knew I stepped off for a minute. Damn, y'all didn't even notice that I was missing,"

"Girl I noticed you were missing with all that ass how could I not?"

I got quiet and brushed it off because we all had been drinking. I walked away, but Rich pulled me back toward him.

"Hold up Rich you drunk and you know Shunda is my best friend,"

He grabbed my ass and told me, "If you won't tell. I won't tell,"

I kissed him and our tongues danced inside each other mouth. I felt his dick print from his shorts. His dick was hard. I went to unbuckle his Gucci belt and pulled his dick out. Damn, he had a big dick just like my best friend said. I got on my knees and sucked my best friend's man dick. He nutted and I swallowed it up and we went back out there with everyone else. We haven't stopped fucking ever since. Shunda never was aware of us creeping. We would get up with each other at the oddest times and places. We had to go far out to meet up just so no one would see us. I never really worked, so I was always available. Shunda worked during the day so those were the best times for us to creep off. Some of Shunda's family members tried to put in her head that she needed to watch me around her man. At first she listened to them and stayed her distanced from me. Then one day Rich bought her a ring and she called me to share the good news. At the same time Rich had bought me a bracelet but I lied and said that some nigga I was fucking with did. Pretty soon all the fucking that Rich and I did caused me to get pregnant.

During that time, I was fucking Ant too. That's why I was pissed off when he lied and told Kelly that he had slept with me only once. Ant stayed creeping off over here and in this pussy. I tried to become his woman but he wasn't going because of my reputation. I was a bad bitch, being light-skinned, thick, and I kept myself up. I was about my money and didn't mess with a nigga who wasn't going to spend it on me. You wasn't fucking me for free. Everything that I got came from a man; even though I was the only child my parents, really couldn't afford to buy me things. So at the age of fourteen, I was sucking and fucking to get the things that I wanted.

I was fucking for hairdos, clothes, phones, cars, bills, purses, jewelry, and money. I thought telling Ant that I was pregnant by him would keep him around. But that shit didn't work and when he got with Kelly, that bitch took him away. I'm not going to lie Rich knew he was the father the whole time, but that couldn't come out since that was my best friend's man. Rich and I slowed it down but he would still keep in touch with me. One day I called Rich so that he could meet me at the doctor's office. I was seven months pregnant and I wanted him to be here with me .I called him several times but Rich never answered. Rich called back; well at least I thought it was him.

I answered, "Rich baby I'm at the doctor's office please come up here with me,"

Shunda laughed and said, "Bitch, Rich ain't coming no damn where, you a dirty hoe!"

I hung up the phone. Shunda called me back but I didn't answer. She sent a voicemail to my phone…….

"I'm going to kill you bitch and that baby when I see you. How could you do this to me? I thought you were my best friend. Everyone warned me about you but I didn't listen. You ain't shit; smiling in my face and you fucking my man. You dirty bitch. You always wanted to be me when were younger. I still called you my friend despite what others thought of you. You always have been a hating ass hoe that couldn't stand to see no one else happy. You want him you can have him and deal with all the bullshit that I have to deal with. Ebony, when I see you I'm fucking you up I don't care if you pregnant or not. I'm beating that baby out of you. It might not even be Rich's baby anyway you whore,"

I left the doctor office and didn't even go home and went straight to my father house. I couldn't go back there because I knew Shunda was going to be there. My phone was ringing like crazy. My male cousin called and told me what Shunda and her cousins did to my apartment. Shunda stop fucking with Rich and kept everything because it was in her name. Rich was fucked up and tried to get back with her, but she didn't take him back. She cut him off from his children and everything. I know she really hated me when she found out for sure that Rich was indeed my baby father. That meant our children were brothers and sisters. I felt bad about how everything turned out with my father and Rich being killed. I couldn't worry about the past. I had to worry about staying alive. Anthony was still after me and with the bounty on my head everyone was after me. Plus, I still had to worry about Shunda. I haven't seen her in five months and I didn't want to see her either.

Chapter 11
Smooth

Rochelle was trying her best to keep me away from my daughter Erica. It has been two months since I've seen her. I was chilling with my peoples one day when someone showed me a picture of Rochelle and her friend Porsha at the club. They were doing some very provocative poses; kissing one another, grabbing each other's ass, and dancing on one another. Don't get me wrong I love two thick bitches, but this heifer Rochelle was back to her partying ways again. If she was out partying, who was watching Erica? Partying is the number one reason why I couldn't cuff Rochelle. She was smart, beautiful, and could light up a room. She just was a party girl and I can't fuck with a chick that goes out to party three times a week. Her and her girls partied so much that they were VIP. Now that I know she was back club hopping I went over to get my daughter. When I got to Rochelle's place, she wasn't there and the babysitter was watching Erica. I asked the babysitter where was Rochelle, she told me that she had gone out and haven't made it home yet.

It was the afternoon; I was boiling and took my daughter with me. The babysitter tried to stop me, but I told her that I would smack her ass. She picked up the phone to dial 911 and I looked at her and she didn't bother to call. Erica was at home with me, at first I didn't plan on keeping her but when my daughter told me she was hungry, that damn near made me wanna kill that bitch Rochelle. She out there partying and shit, and your mutherfucking baby hungry. Then she calls herself a nurse taking care of other people and shit. I took my daughter to home to feed her and she ate the food like she has eaten in days. Ciara just shook her head and walked off. I wanted to cry. Then Rochelle comes to my house banging on the door and shit, looking high and drunk. My daughter really wasn't going back to live with her. I called up my lawyer and told him everything that was going on. I was going to fight to get custody of my daughter. Fuck her. She wasn't going to neglect my child and stop me from seeing her. My lawyer got on it.

We went to court and I had my lawyer and Rochelle had her lawyer. Rochelle bought up that I was a drug dealer and that my home was raided. I denied being a drug dealer and presented to the judge all three of my businesses that I own and as well as properties. The Fed case was thrown out because they couldn't find shit on me. My lawyer was able to get the police report on the day she was arrested at my house. During her arrest they found drugs and alcohol in her system. I presented the pictures as well of Rochelle at the club. I also paid the babysitter to come to court to tell the judge how often she watched Erica. Rochelle was shocked to see the babysitter on my side. Money talks and would buy you what you want. The judge gave me temporary custody and ordered Rochelle to take parenting classes for thirty days. She was mad and cursed me out and tried to fight me after court. That was the reason why I told Ciara not to come because I didn't need the both of them to be fighting.

The first week Rochelle came by my house trying to act a fool and shit. I didn't want to call the police on her. One of my neighbors did and she got in her car and left. She was calling our phones all types of crazy times at night. She even went to my mother's house crying. She had totally lost it. By the second week, we never heard from her again. I guess she couldn't get anyone to feel sorry for her. When I was out late we rode past the party and seen Rochelle and her girls going inside. She was back clubbing I see. I didn't say anything and kept on riding. We put Erica in daycare and we made her feel welcomed in our home. I loved

Ciara because she never showed a difference when it came to Erica or Junior. Thirty days came and I went back to court but Rochelle didn't show up. The judge waited to see if she was running late but she never came. I was awarded full custody of my daughter. I guess Rochelle didn't feel like having the responsibility of being a mother.

Word got around quick that she was partying and that she is a Fun girl. A fun girl is a girl that likes to have sex with girls as well with guys, but they not a lesbian. I don't know why Rochelle wants to live like that, but she lost all respect for me when she stopped fighting for her child. I had more problems to deal with. Kayla was still in custody and had to do a year for the guns that they found in her house during the raid. They wanted to give her five years but my lawyer fought hard. She told me some fucked up news and I can't get myself out of this jam. I kept money on her books and she wrote me through Corr Links. I tried to check back in with her whenever I could. We didn't say much she would let me know that she was cool and that everything was going fine. I couldn't turn my back on her and leave her out there bad. I'm not built that way. She needed me now more than ever.

Ciara

Now it was Smooth, Erica, and junior all under one roof it didn't bother me and I was happy to have Erica to stay with us. At first it was hard and Erica cried for her mommy. She also didn't want anyone but her Father. It was normal, so I didn't let that bother me. It's hard for a child to go from one living situation to another. Trust me, I know and I've been through it. At night time she didn't want to sleep by herself, so Smooth would always sleep on the floor in the bedroom. She asked me one day if her Mommy was ever coming back, I told her yes, and that her mommy loves her. I told Smooth that he needed to spend as much time with her as he could. She got along with Junior and was happy that she had a little brother. They both would play together all day long. Junior was busy walking and getting into everything and Erica was busy helping him. They were both like their father, always getting in some mess.

Today I was chilling with Kelly. I went over to her place to kick back and to get away from the children. I left Smooth at home and told him that I would holler at them later. I needed a break. Lately I've been so busy with getting my new boutique running and planning our wedding. Yes, Smooth and I were still getting married after all the craziness. I had time invested in this man and most of all I love him. I made it to Kelly's in thirty minutes. We caught up on the latest gossip and went to go visit Jasmine. We stopped off first to get some flowers. We made it there and we both laughed and talked to Jasmine like she was here. Before we left we cried and told Jasmine how much we missed her and that we will be back to visit her next month. Didn't anything stop us from visiting our best friend, no rain, hail, sleet, or snow.

Erica's second birthday came around and Smooth had a big party for her at the park. She had a clown, pony rides, jumping jack, magician, and a bunch of other entertainment. He invited Erica's grandparents and her mother, but neither attended. I wasn't surprised that her grandparents didn't show up, because they never cared for Smooth. I was shocked that Rochelle didn't come to her only child birthday party. The day went on and she didn't even call. Smooth was upset, but he didn't let Erica see it. Later on that night Erica came in our bedroom and asked why her mother wasn't there. Smooth didn't know what to say.

Rochelle

Today was my daughter birthday and I was too embarrassed to even show up. I was sitting in the house alone and sniffing coke. I had a minor setback. Due to all the partying, it interfered with my work. I was coming in late, calling off, and when I was there I had a nasty attitude. That caused me to get a lot of write ups and suspensions. As a nurse I had to be there to care for the sick and the ill and have compassion. I almost got fired, but I had to fuck my manager in order to keep my job. I was on a leave of absence now. I missed my baby girl so much but I just couldn't face Smooth and Ciara. I hate them with a passion. I got up and made myself shower and put on some clothes. I was going out with some random man that I met in one of the parties. I didn't care what we did or where we went as long as I was in his arms by the end of the night. My parents stop talking to me. They said I was an embarrassment to the family. Fuck them, I don't care they always worried about what others think or said. That's why they were still unhappily married living under one house but sleeping in separate beds. I wanted to call to check on Erica and to say hello.

Dinner was great and we ended up back at his place. I undressed but before I fucked him I decided to call my daughter. I know it was late at quarter after 12. I called Smooth phone and he answered.

"Hello. Can I speak to Erica?"

"She's sleeping right now. Where were you? She asked about you all day Rochelle,"

"Smooth I don't feel like arguing, I just want to speak with my daughter,"

I heard Ciara say something and Smooth told me to hold on. Moments later Erica got on the phone.

"Mommy, Mommy is this you?"

"Yes baby it's me,"

I started to cry.

"Mommy misses you and loves you sweetie. Happy Birthday baby", she cut me off.

"Mommy why didn't you come to my party, I saved a piece of cake for you,"

"Oh you did. How was the party?"

Erica talked and told me all about the party. She told me who all was there and what gifts she got. She told about her school and her little brother. She told me how Ciara took her to the beauty shop to get her hair and nails done. She went on and on until she told me she was sleepy and had to go because she had a long day tomorrow. I laughed at my baby girl. I told her that I love her and I will be there to see her soon. Smooth got back on the phone and I told him thank you. He hung up on me.

Kayla

I was in downtown Metropolitan Correctional Center in Chicago. I had to do 365 days due to them finding three illegal guns inside the house during the raid. I was blessed that I only got 365 days. I was facing five years. Smooth's lawyers did a excellent job representing me. I talked to Smooth all the time and he kept money on my books. I was happy that he didn't turn my back on me especially when I hit him with the news that I was pregnant. When I got locked up I found out that I was six weeks pregnant. I didn't believe them because I still got my period on a regular. When I first found out I cried and didn't know what to do. I had to fight a case and hope that they didn't put me away for a long time. Now that I was sentenced, I had to just worry about the baby. They provided the healthcare and they were great. It was just fucked up that I will have my baby in here. At first I didn't want to keep it and on several attempts tried to kill it. No matter what the baby never died. When Smooth heard the news he was mad at first, not because I was pregnant, but because I was locked up and pregnant. He never doubted that he was the father because of all the fucking we were doing. He promised me that when I came home that I would be straight and that the baby and I didn't have to worry about shit. He would already have a place for me to stay. That was good because I lost my Section 8 because of the raid and now I have a background.

I talked to him earlier today and he was with Vell. I talked to Vell too. Vell's girlfriend, Aaliyah, has been there for me as well. She would come and visit me all the time. At first I felt that she wasn't sincere and was just coming to see me and report everything back to Smooth. But after getting to know her she was pretty cool. She started off just like me being Vell's side chick and holding shit and being there for him. Another reason why we clicked so well is because she didn't really rock with Ciara. Her cousin Felicia had a fight with Ciara when she was in the group home and that's why Aaliyah stayed her distance from Ciara. Today I was asking to see the doctor because I was having some discomfort. When I got there and told him what was going on he decided to send me to County Hospital to get an ultrasound just to be on the safe side. I was so happy to finally get some fresh air. Even though I was still chained up and heavily guarded.

When I got there I didn't have to wait and the ultrasound was performed. Everything was normal the doctor said that I had gas and prescribed me something. The doctor also told me that I was nineteen weeks and that the sex organs of the baby had formed and that I was having a girl. I cried as I listened to my baby's heartbeat and couldn't wait to tell Smooth that we were having a baby girl. As soon as I got back I went and logged on Corr Links and told him; it's a girl!

Brenda

It was my weekend off and I was at Ciara's place watching the children. I came over last night. Ciara and Smooth went away to a resort for the weekend to get away. I didn't mind doing anything for my daughter I was blessed to be a mother again for the second time. I've been doing great and still working and staying away from alcohol. I moved to a better area on the west side and got myself a car. I had to get out of K town they were doing too much shooting. One day I was in the house and someone tried to break in my house through the back door. My son-in-law Smooth and his friends had to come over there and threaten the boys from around there. It was crazy. I started going back to church. I tried to get Smooth and Ciara to go with me; they would always tell me one Sunday they would come.

Tomorrow I was taking the kids to church with me and they were happy to go. Erica woke up from her nap and walked in the living room asking me if today was Sunday, and was it time for her to get ready for church. I laughed at the child and told her, "No sweetheart today is still Saturday,"

I told her to get the things for her hair so that I could comb it. Junior was still sleeping and I was watching a movie on Lifetime. I was combing Erica hair and having flashbacks of the times when I used to comb Ciara hair. I was so evil back then I couldn't believe the things that I used to do. Thank God that I have come a long way. I finished combing Erica hair and she ran to the mirror to look at it. She came back in the living room and told me she liked her hair so much. Junior woke up and came walking in the living room. Erica ran up to Junior showing him hair and he tried to pull her hair.

"Boy, let your sister hair go", I said.

I fed them and then went back to watching Lifetime. Someone rung the door bell and I went to see who it was. I opened up the door and it was Rochelle, Erica's mother.

"How can I help you?" I asked

"Hey, is ok for me to see Erica. I just wanted to take her out for a little while and spend some time with her,"

"Eric isn't here at the moment maybe you should come back then", I went to close the door, but she put her foot in the way.

"Look you old bitch, let me see my baby!"

I stepped off and on to the porch and got directly in her face.

"Don't let my age fool you. I will fuck you up. Now take your loose ass somewhere before I kick your ass all up and down this street,"

She turned to walk away. I stared at her and didn't go back inside until she got in her car and drove off. I stepped back in the house and said, "Lord please forgive me!"

Chapter 12
Ciara

Smooth and I had reservations at Eaglewood Resort & Spa. We needed to get away and I needed to get pampered. I was happy that my mother came over to watch the kids for the weekend. We kissed them good bye and was off to the resort. We had the rooftop suite. It was big and beautiful. It had its own private staircase and was separate from the main building. A flat panel TV was on the wall, a king sized bed, and we had a fireplace.

"Thank you so much baby, I needed this with all the bullshit that's been going on,"

"Anything for you Blackbone; you know how much I love you baby,"

I kissed him and Smooth took out his blunt and weed and started rolling up.

"You smoke anywhere", I laughed.

I opened up the Patron and poured him a glass.

"Thanks baby", he said.

Smooth got comfortable as I unpacked our things. It was Friday night and raining outside. I went to run the water in the Jacuzzi and when it was ready we both got inside. Smooth begged me to take a sip of Patron. I took one sip and that shit was strong. He laughed and told me to drink some more. I drank a cup of Patron and turned into another person. I sucked Smooth dick under water. He was going crazy and loving that shit. When I was done I sat on the ledge of the Jacuzzi as Smooth ate my pussy. I pushed his head deeper inside my pussy. I wanted to feel all his tongue and tried to smother him. We got back in the water and I began to surf board his dick. He pulled my hair as I popped my pussy on his dick. I got out the water and on all fours and Smooth fucked me from behind. I looked back at my ass and watched it jingle. Smooth kissed me roughly and grabbed my hips and I threw my ass back on his dick.

"Oh shit this pussy so good I'm about to nut? Where do you want this nut baby? Tell daddy where you want this nut at?"

"Nut in my mouth daddy,"

Smooth pulled out and I turned around and started sucking his dick. Moments later his hot sperm shoot down my throat and I swallowed it all up.

The next morning we both woke up on the floor. My head was banging. I tried to get up but I was dizzy. Smooth got up and gave me some

Advil. We showered and did a quickie and went down to the spa. At the spa the package I picked was "*The Queen for the Day*". I was given a facial, massage, manicure, pedicure, mud wrap, and many parts of my body waxed. Smooth got a massage, manicure and pedicure. After we were done getting pampered, we ate at the restaurant. I had lobster, salmon with a side of mashed potatoes and a glass of wine. Smooth had steak, lobster, mac & cheese, baked potato and a glass of Hennessy. Once we were finished, we went back to our suite, and it was time for me to make love to my man. We both got naked and this time we used the bed.

It was Monday morning and time for us to get back home to the kids. Smooth and I had a great time and we stayed inside all day Sunday with no interruptions. It was after 9 a.m. when we walked in the door. My mother had taken Erica and Junior to daycare and was watching Lifetime sitting on the couch.

"Hey momma, we home", I said and gave her a kiss.

Smooth did the same and went in the back to put our bags away.

"I hope the children didn't drive you crazy and give you any problems,"

"Oh no, the children were fine and they had a good time at church. The only problem I had was when Erica's mother, Rochelle, came by here!"

My mother told Smooth and I what happened and I was livid. I ran outside and jumped in car. Smooth and my mother were yelling at me to come back but I ignored them. It took me twenty minutes to get to Rochelle's house. She was outside getting groceries out of her car. I ran up on her and punched that bitch so hard in her mouth. She dropped her food and for the first time she was trying her best to fight me back. She still couldn't beat me. I grabbed that bitch by her throat and was giving her straight face shots. She was swinging her arms and had grabbed a little bit of my hair. I punched her and slammed her ass to the ground. I started kicking her in her mouth and then out of nowhere, Smooth grabbed me. The police came and I was arrested and charged. I heard Rochelle was in the hospital with a broken arm, a jaw, and I knocked three teeth out of her mouth. I didn't give a fuck I don't play about my mother.

Kelly

I had a chance to finally talk to my brother Shawn. I told all about being engaged to Anthony and he was happy for me. He was doing well in California, making a lot of cash, and told me that he wasn't coming back to live in Chicago. He was giving me both of his buildings and told me that he would still pay for my education. I was sad at first, but I understood why he did it. I told him that I loved him and that Anthony and I was coming to see him during Christmas or either New Year. He spoke to Anthony on the phone for about forty minutes. I knew they were talking business because as soon as Anthony got off the phone with him, he called Smooth, Vell, and Red and told them he was calling a meeting. I didn't know what was going on because Anthony never shared his business with me when it came to the streets. That was one of his rules. The less I know the better.

I got up and went to go handle my business downtown to meet with Shawn's lawyer and got the properties in my name. After that, I and my grandma went out to eat at MacArthur's Restaurant. She loved their soul food. We chatted and she was happy that I finally talked to my brother. I was happy too. Once we were done, we went to the mall and I got my grandma some church clothes and hats. All she did was go to church. That was her life. Since it was Wednesday, I went to bible study with her. She was so happy. It was good to be back in church. I wondered if I could get Anthony to go with me. When I got home, I called Anthony to come outside to get the bags. I jumped in the tub and soaked my body. I was tired from all that running around.

The next day Ciara, her mother, Smooth's mother and I went to go look at bridal and bridesmaid dresses. I think we went to over ten different stores until she finally saw the dress that she wanted. Ciara went to try it on and came back. She looked beautiful and everyone started to cry. She started crying because she saw us crying. She picked that dress and purchased it. Next it was time for us to try on dresses. That was crazy after an hour we all agreed on something and left the bridal shop. I was tipsy and horny, thanks to the people at the bridal shop who served us wine. I called Anthony and told him that I was ready to ride his dick all night and please don't be late coming in. I took a few naked pictures and sent it to his phone.

He called me back and said, "Baby why you do that to me, now I can't even concentrate,"

I laughed and told him I was sorry, and that I would be home waiting for him and that I love him.

He said, "I love you too,"

The fellas laughed and made fun of him in the background. I told them all to shut up and hung up the phone.

Smooth

I was reading Kayla message and she was telling me that she was having a girl. I had to get her situated and find a place for her and the baby. I don't know how the fuck I was going to pull this one off. Ciara wasn't going to be too happy if she found out about this child. I wasn't worried about Kayla, because now she got me right where she wants me. I was going to look out for her under the circumstances of her doing time for me and didn't snitch. I will always love her for that. If it would have been Rochelle, she would have told everything; I kind of felt as though she had something to do with the FBI raid, but I couldn't prove it. If she did, I would kill her myself. I hate that bitch and I've never hated a woman before. Ciara fucked her up really bad for disrespecting her mother. We haven't heard shit from her since then. She didn't even come to court and the charges were dropped from Ciara. I was happy that my baby wasn't charged with any felonies. We were still looking for Ebony and my cousin Toby said he hadn't seen her. I'm quite sure that she will pop up soon. I saw Rich's baby momma, Shunda, in my bar the other night and she said that she was looking for her too. She showed me her gun, that girl is straight gangsta. I don't know why Rich was fucking with Ebony scary ass for. That nigga let some pussy get him killed.

Shunda was cool because she had an insurance policy on him. I told her once we find her I would let her know. Ciara was getting prepared for our wedding. After everything we were still getting married. I love Ciara and decided to wife her. I'm the only man she has ever been with and I couldn't see her with another nigga. I know I'm not shit and out here fucking around but no woman comes before her. It's hard for a man to just fuck one female. I'm young and out here getting money. I'm not wild I'm just enjoying life. We were going to spend our honeymoon in Hawaii. Anthony had an idea to work with Shawn down in California. I was down, we already had a Texas connect; more money for the whole team. We were going to hang out at the bar tonight; the city been fucking with me, so I had to pay them off to keep them off my ass.

Shit been crazy out here and everyone was trying to get money, but not willing to put the work in. I had a few cats that tried us, but they didn't live to tell their stories. I was sitting in the office and thinking about the days when Vell, Ant, Red and I was fourteen and hustling, now we had our own shit. We did a lot of dirt together that we all taking it to the grave. We fucked bitches together, popped bottles together, and we would forever make money together. I was disturbed by a phone call from Kayla; I answered and talked to her. She really missed a nigga and I missed her too and that pussy. I told her that she was gonna be straight and I got her. She always told me that she loved me, but I never said it back. I had love for her but I wasn't in love with her; big difference. Ciara has been the only woman that I've loved besides my mother. Don't get me wrong, now that she is having my child I would fuck a nigga up if they came wrong at her.

Kayla talked freaky on the phone. She will never change that, she was a super freak and she became a selfish one for me. In the beginning, she was crazy but I don't blame her because I was seeing her before Ciara. So I could understand why she was acting crazy. She still didn't like that I was getting married. I told her if I could have the both of them under one roof I would. Ciara wasn't going for that.

Ebony

I woke up from a nightmare and checked to see if Kimora was still lying next to me. She was still there and I was still alive. I had a nightmare that they found me and killed me and my baby. It was 6 a.m. and I wasn't even going back to sleep. I stayed up and watched TV. I got up to count my money and noticed it was getting low. I had to get a job really soon. I didn't have any skills and I only had a high school diploma. I wasn't working for anyone just making pennies. I got up and looked in the mirror to check out my body. I still had it and looked good to have a six month old. I could tighten up some things. Give me four weeks and I will be back in the game and I bet you I will win first place.

Kimora woke up and I fed her after that my phone rang. It had to be my cousin, he was the only one that had my number and knew where I was. My cousin was Mario aka Rio. He was my first cousin on my mother's side. He was a nigga from the streets and he stayed up north in Chicago. He went back and forth out of town a lot and didn't hang with a lot of niggas. He told me everything that was going on in Chicago. Shunda was living large off the insurance policies that she had on Richard aka Rich. She was still looking for me and had people out there looking for me too. She wanted me dead. Anthony aka Ant was still looking for me and had a bounty on my head. Ant was also getting married to Kelly next year. I was mad when I heard that. I hated Kelly and I can't believe that Ant was marrying that skinny bitch.

Ant and his team were making major moves. Fuck, how I wish he was my baby daddy now more than ever. That Kelly was a lucky bitch. The shocking news that I wasn't prepared to hear is that my mother stayed down here in Dallas with her third husband. So my mother got married again. Rio said that he talked to his mother, his mother and mine are sisters and she told him that my mother was down here. My mother and father had a messy divorce when I was seventeen years old. She left and ran off but my father wouldn't allow her to take me. I stayed in Chicago and when I was older I talked to her sometimes. The last I spoke with her I was twenty years old, three years ago. She was married to a man and they both lived in Minnesota. I had no idea that she remarried. He gave me her number and address. I thanked him for the information and told him to call me if he hears anything new.

Kimora and me went to Target to buy a few things. I bought some things to help me get in shape and some more personal items. Dallas was cool and everyone was so polite. I liked living down here. Maybe I could start all over; you know, maybe go back to school and get me a nigga. Maybe in the future, I thought, but not right now I had to try to stay alive. I stopped by a local pawn shop and looked at the guns. I wasn't allowed to get one legally so I paid this white boy to get one for me. I went back home and cooked dinner for me and Kimora.

The next day I was working out to the DVD that I had bought. Kimora was in her swing looking at me. I was laughing at my baby. I was determined to get my body back in shape. Momma needs a job baby. I was going to give stripping a try. Once I was finished working out, I turned on some music and started to practice dancing. I had to learn how to twerk. I went on You Tube and followed the instructions of the girl who was giving the lesson. It was pretty easy. I already had enough ass and a little rhythm. With a lot more practice I would be ready to at least give a lap dance.

For the next several weeks working out and dancing became my daily routine. I had to make some real money and fast. Plus, maybe I can find a nigga down here that got cash.

Chapter 13
Rochelle

I sat back from a distance and watched the guests enter the church. Today was the day of Ciara and Smooth's wedding. People gathered inside so I knew the ceremony had to be happening soon. After everything I did to destroy their relationship, they were still together and getting married. I was crazy in love with Smooth. I missed my baby girl and she looked just like her father. She was beautiful and deserves to have me and Smooth, not Ciara and Smooth. Instead, he wants to be with a hood chick. Not a real woman. So what she owned a damn boutique. What did that mean, with them wack-ass clothes. I had a degree and a real career. I was a nurse and I owned my home and only drove foreign. To make matters worse, he had taken my daughter away from me. I hated Ciara and that's why I planned on interrupting her wedding. I had a surprise for them. They would always remember this day.

I walked inside the church and the lovely assistant greeted me and gave me a wedding program. I stood outside the door first before I entered inside. I was disguised. I had on a short black wig and black frames on. I had on an all black dress. I went inside and had a seat in the back. The wedding was about to start. Some lady started singing *At Last*. She was cool, but damn they could have picked another song. The wedding party came down the aisle. My daughter was the prettiest flower girl that I have seen. A tear trickled down my face. The music changed and they organist played. *Here Comes The Bride*. I looked at Smooth's smiling ass. He won't be smiling for long, I thought. Ciara came down the aisle. All eyes were on her. She looked beautiful in her all white gown. She won't be pretty for long not when I'm done. By the time she made it to the altar, Smooth was crying. He was really putting on a show. I laughed at his clown ass. The pastor began talking. We are gathered here today blah, blah, blah. I sighed I was waiting on my moment. Finally he spoke.

"If any man can show just cause why they should not be lawfully be joined together, let them speak now or else here after forever hold his peace,"

I stood up and said, "I do!"

Everyone turned and looked at me amazed.

"You two ruined my life and took my daughter away from me. I hate the both of you. Smooth you won't be marrying that bitch today,"

I walked down the aisle and removed my shades and wig. Smooth nodded his head. Security came rushing toward me. I removed my gun. Everyone in the church got low.

"Mommy", I heard my baby girl Erica say.

"It's okay baby, Momma is here to take you home", I pointed my gun at Smooth.

"All I ever did was love you and you played me like a fool. Now you up here marrying this bitch,"

"You Bitch", said Ciara.

I pointed the gun towards Ciara

"Shut the fuck up bitch before I push your shit back," Smooth told her to be quiet.

"Yeah, she better be quiet. Bitch it's my time to talk,"

The pastor tried to get me to put the gun down.

"Shut the fuck up and go to hell. I don't want to hear all that God loves you bullshit. Fuck God!"

"Put the gun down Rochelle, we can talk about this. Think about what you are doing in front of your daughter. Look at her crying she doesn't need to see you like this", Smooth said.

I looked over at my baby girl crying. She looked so beautiful. She ran over to Ciara which only made me madder. All I saw was red. I pointed my gun at Ciara.

"Get your hands off my daughter. You already have my man and now you trying to take my daughter too", Ciara released Erica.

"Come to momma Erica,"

"No!" Smooth yelled Erica cried and didn't know what to do.

"Come to momma", I said.

"Erica, come to daddy", she looked at the both of us and ran back to her daddy.

You turned my own daughter against me. I fucking hate you and that bitch. I hope you rot in hell", I pulled the trigger *POW! POW! POW!*

Everyone screamed and ran out of the church. I fell to floor I had been hit. I grabbed my chest and blood was everywhere, gasping for air I cried out help. I could hear several voices, but I heard Erica crying, "Mommy, Mommy!" I was becoming weaker and everything became dark. My last words were, "I Love You Erica!"

Please enjoy a Sneak Peek of my new novel, "Sneaky Pussy"

Dirty Bitches Be Plotting

Chapter One

I met King one day in traffic. I was on my way to the bank to make a deposit. While sitting at the light a black Benz pulled on the side of me. I glanced over to my right to check the car out. It was nice and one day I was gonna own me one. He smiled and I smiled back. The light turned green and I pulled off. I made it to the bank; I ran inside to handle my business and walked back out. When

I stepped out I noticed the black Benz parked next to my Camry.

"Excuse me beautiful what is your name?" he asked.

"Look I'm sorry and I'm not really in a good mood today." I said.

"You too beautiful of a woman to let anything make you upset."

"Well thank you."

"Ok maybe he's not such a jerk after all."

I got in my car and he asked, "So are you going to tell me your name?"

"My name is Amerie."

"That's a beautiful name it fits you."

"Thank you."

"Well Amerie do you mind if I can take you out one day?"

"Sure what is your name?"

"They call me King." He said and flashed me a smile.

We exchanged numbers and agreed to talk later.

I called King that night and found out that he was 29 years old. He had one daughter and he was no longer with the mother of his child. He was a dope man and we were both from the same side of town. I didn't know him because I was a home body and didn't really run the streets that much. I told him that I was 21; no kids, single, and that I had a customer service job. I worked Monday thru Friday, so we set up a date on Saturday.

I met King at the restaurant. He insisted on picking me up but I didn't feel comfortable with him knowing where I stayed. Dinner was great; we had steak, lobster, and crab legs. King was older and I loved me an older man; they know how to treat a lady. Men my age wasn't on shit. King was the type of man that I needed in my life.

I made it home and called him to let him know that I made it in safely. We stayed on the phone until 3a.m. just talking about everything.

Monday morning I went to work and was having a terrible day. King texted me and asked how my day was going. I told him shitty and that Monday's have never been a good day for me. An hour later a young man came in with a boutique of flowers and asked for me. I was so happy, they were beautiful. I opened up the card and read it.

If I have to send you flowers every Monday to make it wonderful I will. I smiled and hurried and called King back and thanked him for the flowers. When I got home I called King and we talked again until I fell asleep. The weekend came and I invited him to my house. He came in and sat on the couch as I got ready.

"Nice apartment for a young girl", he said.

"Thanks I try to keep it together."

We left and King threw me his keys and let me drive the Benz. I drove him around all day. We went to the car wash. That's when I found out that King owned the carwash. It was a popular spot that every local dope boy came and got their whips washed. I had to put my girls on to this. Next we went out to eat downtown. After that he took me shopping and let me pick out whatever I wanted. It was getting late and I didn't want the day to end. King asked me to go back to his place and I said yes. We made it to King house and it was really nice.

"You better not tell anyone where I stay", he said.

"I promise not to tell anyone where you stay, you can trust me."

He showed me around and the last room was the bedroom. He had a king size bed fit for a King. I fucked King that night like a porn star. I wanted to I'm not going to lie. Besides he has been too nice to me and spent a lot of money on me. I felt that he had earned it. In the morning I fucked him again.

"I knew you were a little freak; the good girls are the freakiest ones."

I bit down on my lip and said, "Good girl gone bad."

We both laughed and I went back to sucking his dick. We went to breakfast in the morning and came back to the house to continue fucking. I woke up in an empty bed and noticed King wasn't there. I heard voices coming from downstairs. I jumped in the shower got dressed and went to join

King. When I walked downstairs I noticed King had company.

"I see someone has finally woken up."

"Yes I like to get my beauty rest." I sat down next to him on the couch.

His friend watched me. King introduced the both of us.

"This is my good friend Ace. Ace this is my girl Amerie."

"Hello, how are you?" I said.

"I'm cool." Ace said.

I sat there for a moment while they both discussed business. I could see that Ace really didn't seem too comfortable with me hearing them talk, so I politely removed myself to give them more privacy. Once King was done and Ace left King and I watched movies and hung out the rest of the weekend. I was starting to like King he wasn't like the thirsty men my age. The weekend was over and I had to go to work in the morning. He took me home and I kissed him goodnight inside the car before I went inside. We promised to call one another tomorrow.

Chapter Two

Things were going great with King and me. We were going back and forth on dates. Back and forth out of town just spending a lot of time together. He introduced me to a few of his buddies. From there my girls and his guys were starting to hang out. We were hitting parties and having a good time. I wasn't used to this type of lifestyle. I was the girl who used to go to work and back. I didn't do anything but stay in the house and read books. King and I were starting to get a lot of attention around town. Some people felt that King didn't have any business dealing with a girl that was eight years younger than him. Plus they said that I was just a gold digger and was just using him. I laughed I didn't care what people had to say. I was in love with King. He showed me a different world and introduced me to the finer things in life. Besides when you deal with an older man he is supposed to upgrade and uplift you. That's exactly what King did and I was happy.

On my 22nd birthday King surprised me with a new car. He bought me a Lexus. I was so happy and I wasn't even expecting it. I snatched the car keys out of his hands and hit the streets. I called up my friends and picked them up. They were happy for me. We rode around town and everyone watched me spinning and grinning. By next week I was the talk of the town. Hoes hated big time. They were jumping out of the bushes trying to find out who I was fucking with just so they can fuck with him and get some money. I brought King's pussy radar up. I wasn't worried about my baby cheating on me. He was so busy getting money.

King told me to meet him in the city at some apartment. I pulled up and called him to let him know that I was outside. He told me to come in. A little girl let me in. I went inside the place it was nicely decorated and King was in the back. I sat down and King and Ace came in the front.

"Hey baby, you cool you need anything?" King asked.

"Hey and no I'm fine."

I spoke to Ace as him and King continued to conduct busy. Moments later a brown skinned skinny girl with long weave down hair back came from out of a bedroom carrying a bag. She walked passed me and went to sit on Ace lap and dropped the cash out of the bag. I figured she was Ace girl. She didn't pay me any attention. I pulled out my phone to play Candy crush and the noise from the game got King attention.

"You addicted to that damn game?" King said.

"Yes, besides it's nothing else to do but sit here and watch you." I said a little irritated.

"I'm sorry baby, give me a minute and I will be done."

They continued to count the money. I asked where was the bathroom and the girl pointed to the back. I went to use it and on my way back walking in the hallway I peeped inside a room. I saw a picture of Ace and the girl in a frame. I went to sit back down and was happy that King was ready to go. We left and he passed me the bag of money and told me to keep it at my place. At first I didn't agree but he talked me into it.

The next week King called me and asked me could I do him a favor? I said yes. He wanted me to meet Ace to pick up a package. I went to meet him at the destination and Ace was running late. Finally 20 minutes later a car came and parked behind me. It wasn't Ace but instead it was his girlfriend. She gave me the bag but this time she introduced herself.

"Hi I'm Cassie. You're Amerie right the girl who was at my house last week?"

"Yes I am.' I said dryly.

"Sorry about keeping you waiting, Ace got wrapped up into something so I came instead."

She gave me the bag of money and I talked briefly with her. I wasn't trying to have a long conversation with her ass. I left and called King to curse him out. I was making myself clear to him that this was my last time getting involved with his business. I'm not that type of girl and the less I know the better. We agreed and he promised not to get me involved anymore. I took the bag of money to my house and he promised to meet me there this evening. Hours later he called and had a change of plans and asked me if I would go to the club with him tonight. I was happy and told him yes and that I would be ready.

King and I were partying sitting in VIP and Ace and Cassie joined us. Over the months Ace has grown to be really cool. I found out that Cassie was Ace baby momma and that they had two kids together. She was a kitchen beautician. Cassie talked to me during the party. She was cool but I had my own set of friends and wasn't trying to make new ones. I was drunk and horny and ready to go. I told King lets go home so that I could ride his pole. We left but Ace and Cassie stayed.

During the ride home I pulled King's dick out to give him some head. He leaned back and I swallowed his whole dick in my mouth.

"Damn baby that shit feels good. You are trying to make me tear my shit up."

I smiled and continued licking and sucking on his dick until he busted a nut. I swallowed up all of it. I sat up and opened my legs and slid my panties to the side and started playing with my pussy. King was trying to watch me and the road. I moaned as I fingered my clit. I took my fingers and stuck them in King's mouth. He licked them one by one. I continued playing with my pussy until we got in front of his house. When we got inside King pushed me against the wall and forced his dick in me. He fucked me against the wall until he busted his second nut. He dropped down on his knees and ate my pussy. I was climbing up the wall. I came all over his tongue and gave my baby a kiss.

In the morning I made breakfast for him, and after we ate we fucked again. We showered got dressed and hit the streets. I was happy to be by his side. King made several stops. I was surprised that he stopped by his baby mother house with me in the girl. He had a 15 year old daughter name Brandy. I stayed in the car while King went inside. His baby mother Roxanne wasn't too fond of me being that I was nine years younger than her. To me she had to be jealous because she had moved on and had a new man and everything. And King bought his daughter whatever she needed.

Fifteen minutes later King and Brandy got in the car and we all went shopping. I've never met Brandy before but talked to her on the phone, so she already was aware of me. We clicked pretty well and created a bond. Brandy was spoil. She was only a teenager and rocking Gucci bags already. We were at the mall and King bought her whatever she asked for. Brandy was an A student and on the honor roll so he spoiled her. She was his twin and looked identical to King. We went to eat at The Cheesecake Factory and after that he took her back home. Roxanne was waiting at the door for her daughter to enter. Before Brandy went inside she said, "See you later Daddy, I love you."

She told me, "See you later Amerie."

Before I could respond back Roxanne slammed the door closed.

Chapter Three

Months had gone by. King and I was still an item. I didn't work anymore due to a lay off from my job. King was there to support me. I still had my own apartment, but I spent a lot of time at King's Place. I had keys to the crib. I was known around town as the young girl who was a gold digger and only messed with men with money. That was crazy because King had only been my first real relationship that I had with any man. King was known as the person who the little hustlers had to go through. He had connections all over.

We were always going back in forth down South. He had a lot of family and money down there. His Mother lived down South so that was a major reason we visited quite often.

Where ever he went I was close by his side. I still had my girlfriends and we would hang out every once in a while. I stayed shopping, going to the spa, and just living a lavish lifestyle. Some women were jealous and talked about me like a dog. Some women even plotted on trying to fuck with King on low. Dirty bitches I tell you. King always came back to tell me who to watch. I was never the type of female to run my mouth about what I and my man did in the bedroom. Bitches just had seen how I was living and wanted it too. What women fail to realize is they don't know what I had to do to get his heart. Also just because he treats me great doesn't mean that you would get the same treatment.

I was hanging out with Ace and my cousin Morgan one day. Ace was really cool and low key he was fucking with my cousin Morgan. Ace and Morgan met one day before without my knowledge. I didn't care about him seeing my cousin as long as he treated her right. Cassie didn't know about it and besides she wasn't my friend. I only became friendly with her on the strength of King and Ace. We were all chilling and hanging out at King's Place. King had gone to run some errands and left us alone. We were watching Kevin Hart silly ass on TV. Ace phone rung and we all got quiet. It was Cassie calling him.

"What up?"

"Shit I'm chilling."

"I called you thirty minutes ago and you didn't answer!"

"Had the music up my ass."

"Next time you better answer the phone."

"I will call you back when I'm finished."

Ace seemed a little upset but my cousin Morgan jumped on his lap and started licking his ear. I went back to watching TV and then King walked in. He had some food and everyone jumped up to get the food. I gave him a kiss. We were all eating at the table and talking.

"I just saw Cassie she looking for your ass." King said.

"Man fuck Cassie I just talked to her", said Ace.

We ate the rest of our food and Ace and Morgan crept off in a room to fuck. King and I did the same.

King and I were starting to have little problems, so I decided to give him some space and spend more time at my place. I was hanging out with my girls a lot more often. We were going to parties and going back and forth out of town. I was still King's girl and we will spend as much time together when we could. I even found me a part time job. I was trying to stay busy and not depend on King's money. He still paid my car note and rent, but other than that I still had my own money.

One night I and my girls were out partying. We were having a good time. I see and ran into a lot of people who I haven't seen in a while. Plenty of men tried to push up on me simply because I was a hot item. I wasn't going for it. These niggas wasn't even worth it. My friends and I popped bottle after bottle. I noticed Cassie and her friend in there. They were pretty much off to their selves.

I didn't want to invite her over because Morgan was with me and that would have seemed awkward. This one local hustler kept on trying to push up on me. He wouldn't stop and he was touching on me and everything. I had to check his ass because I didn't even fuck with him like that and I had a man. He knew if King found out that he was doing this he wasn't going to be able talk when he was finished with him. We continued to party and afterwards we went home.

The next day I was awaken by pounding on my door. I didn't know who was pounding on my door. I looked out the peep hole and it was King. I opened up the door and he came storming inside and checking all the rooms.

"What is going on? Who are you looking for?" I asked.

He slammed me up against the wall by my throat.

"Bitch where that nigga at you was talking to last night?"

I was confused because I didn't know what the hell King was talking about. I was crying and scared. I have never seen King act like this before.

I've heard rumors that he used to beat Roxanne, but that was because she used to do spiteful things to him.

"What nigga? I wasn't talking to anyone last night. Can you please stop you're hurting me." I cried.

I see a crazy deranged look in King eyes that I've never seen before. He was really scaring me. He was already bigger than me and could fuck me up. It was just him and me in here and he could do anything to me and no one would ever know. I cried and the tears ran down my face. He dropped me on the floor.

"Bitch I heard you were at the club last night dancing all on a nigga and shit. Ain't no bitch of mine got know damn business disrespecting me."

"First of all I'm not a bitch so you better watch your mouth!"

Smack!

King smacked me so damn hard I seen stars. I didn't believe this nigga just hit me. I got up and ran into my room and grabbed my gun. King starting running when he seen me with my gun in my hand. I fired one shot and missed him. King jumped in his car and rode off. I called Ace to tell him what had just happen and he quickly came over. King was trying to call me several times but I ignored his calls. Ace got to my house and asked me what was going on.

"He came over my motherfucking house this morning banging on the door and shit talking about I was fucking with some nigga last night at the party."

Ace had a look on his face liked he knew what was going on. King called Ace phone and Ace told him that he was with me right now. I didn't want to talk to King anymore I was done with his ass. I've never had a man put his hands on me before. If he did it once he would do it again. Ace tried to get me to talk to him but I wasn't trying to hear that shit.

"I can't believe you shot at him." Ace said laughing. "Damn you crazy as hell."

"Ace you should have seen how hard he smacked me." I said as I was holding a towel of against my face. "That nigga crazy and I swear I wasn't talking to another nigga last night. I wonder who told him that bullshit."

Ace got quiet and just listened to me talk. My phone was ringing constantly. I wasn't talking to anyone at the moment. I had a crazy morning and was trying to figure out who told King that.

Chapter Four

A week had gone by since I've seen or heard from King. He would call me but I didn't answer. Send flowers, cards, and candy to my house. He even came up to my job, but I would leave out the back exit to avoid running into him. Ace would call to check on me. When he did I kept the conversation to a minimum because he was King's friend and not mine. I know he was going back and reporting to King.

The weekend rolled around and I got a call from my cousin Morgan. She was in the house bored and had nothing to do. She suggested that I come over there to hang out and promised to fry me some chicken. I loved her fried chicken. I got dressed and went over there. When I got there Morgan was in the kitchen cooking.

"It smells so good in here. I can't wait till you finish cooking, I'm starving." I said.

Morgan was busy talking on the phone maybe to one of her niggas. She had plenty. Morgan was the man version when it came to relationships. She didn't care about settling down. She didn't have any children and was beautiful. So she was a player and never got played. She got off the phone.

"Cousin hand me the blender so I can make us some strawberry daiquiris." Morgan said.

I gave her the blender and we made our daiquiris. Twenty minutes later her doorbell rang.

"Can you get the door?"

"Bitch I'm a guest you get your own door."

She answered her door. Morgan walked back in the kitchen and I was looking for who came inside the house. Sitting at her kitchen table my eyes bucked when I see it was King. Morgan sneaky ass set me up. I got up from the table and tried to leave out her back door.

"Amerie stop being extra and please at least listen to what he has to say", Morgan said.

"No fuck him and fuck you! He had no business accusing me of some bullshit that I didn't do and putting his hands on me."

I tried my best to leave but Morgan wouldn't allow me. King finally spoke.

"I'm sorry Love. I don't know what got over me. I was so mad when I heard the news and took it out on you. I know the truth now and I promise not to hit you again."

I looked at him before I spoke back. He looked sad and stupid by the face. I can tell that he really missed me because he went through so much to see me. King didn't have to chase me he had enough me to replace me. Deep down inside I missed him too and was tired of dodging him. I decided to give him another chance.

"The next time you put your hands on me again I'm not missing next time." I warned him.

He laughed and called me crazy. I wasn't laughing I was serious I don't play that domestic violence shit. Morgan was standing there watching us like we were a soap opera.

"Ok so you two need to leave and make up." Morgan said.

King hugged me really tight and thanked Morgan. We went to leave but before I left I grabbed a few wings to go.

"Excuse me King, you forgetting something," Morgan said.

King gave Morgan a hundred dollars. I knew my cousin wasn't doing anything for free. She smiled and walked us to the door.

When we made it back to King house I went around the whole entire house searching for any signs of a female. He didn't say shit and I wished he would've. I haven't been with him for a week in a half. You know men can't go long without fucking. Once everything was ok I jumped in the shower. When I got out King was lying down in bed naked.

"Come here baby and sit on Daddy face."

I straddle King's face and he licked my pussy so good.

"Oh my god," I said.

"I miss the taste of your pussy."

He was licking my pussy so good that I was running away from his tongue. Ladies older men can eat the hell out of some pussy. King told me to turn around and started eating my pussy from the back. I rode his face and then I felt his tongue in my ass.

"Damn you showing out Daddy."

That shit felt good. I sucked his dick but I couldn't concentrate because he was eating my ass so good. He asked me something that I wasn't expecting.

"Can I fuck you in the ass?"

"Yes, but don't hurt me."

King put on a condom and lubricated his dick. He stuck the tip in first. That wasn't so bad. He was going deeper but I started running. He told me to relax. He went in deeper slowly. It was painful but I took the pain. He spit on my ass and it trickled down my crack. He went further inside me. I can feel his dick it felt strange. King went in deeper and started pumping slowly some more.

"Yes baby Daddy almost in, just keep on relaxing."

Next thing you know I felt a pain that was of pleasure. He pumped a little faster. I can tell that he was in my ass and enjoying it. I didn't feel anything at first. His dick was swelling up in me. Oh my, what the hell did I get myself into? I just let King have his way with my ass until he busted his nut. Once he was done I ran inside the bathroom and it hurt like hell. I took a towel and cleaned myself up. It was a little bit of blood I heard from my cousin Morgan that was normal. I lay down and went to sleep. King wasn't fucking me anymore tonight.

Keep It On The Down Low

Chapter One

We all sat on the bench in the park and watched the local ball players play basketball. It was Gina, Whitney, Hope, and I. The sun was out and you know what that meant. Everyone was outside enjoying the weather. Children were playing and running around the playground. The snowball stand was posted and making money. The bottle of water that I was drinking was coming to an end.

"I'm going to go and buy me a snowball. Someone walk over there with me."I said.

"Chiquita if I walk with you then you paying for mine."Hope said.

"Girl you don't have a damn dollar to buy a snowball?"I asked.

Hope rolled her eyes. I know I was wrong for saying what I was thinking out loud. Shit I know that both of Hope's parents are out there bad, but damn her grandmother still takes good care of her.

"I would walk with you and come on Hope I will buy you a snowball."Whitney said.

Whitney and I started to walk towards the snowball stand. We were quite a distance from Hope and Gina. Hope didn't bother to get off of the bench so I guess she changed her mind about going.

"Are you coming?"Whitney asked Hope.

 "No I'm going to sit here with Gina since I don't have a dollar."

I didn't feed into it. Instead Whitney and I walked away.

"Girl you know you were wrong for putting Hope on blast like that."Whitney said.

"No I wasn't and I don't care. I know Hope have a dollar she always playing the sympathy role just because her parents out here bad and shit. We out of high school now and that shit doesn't work anymore. Everyone felt sorry for her ass then. She grown now and the bitch need to get a job."

"Let me find out you still mad because she looked better than you on prom bitch."

"Bitch please, she was cool."I rolled my eyes.

To be honest Hope was the bomb on prom. Thanks to all the money and the help that her grandmother had received from church. Hope had a custom made dress. Weave down to her ass, red bottom shoes, and a rented Porsche truck. Her date was the star player of the basketball team, Fred. His parents arranged for the both of them to go on prom together since they were all members at the same church. They were the most talked about at prom and received a lot of attention being that Fred was a star basketball player. I was very jealous. I was feeling Fred on the low. He became off limits once he and Hope went on prom together. He tried to act like he wasn't feeling her but they fucked after prom. We made it to the snowball stand and bought our snowballs. As we were walking back Corey and Lil John pulled up, parked, and jumped out the car to talk shit. Corey was my play brother. We were both the only child. I always wanted a brother and Corey always wanted a sister so we decided to be one another play sister and brother. Lil John was Gina's man; they also had a two year daughter together. I remember when Gina got pregnant. That was the talk of the town. Everyone thought that she was going to drop out and thought that Lil John wasn't going to take care of his child. They proved everyone wrong. Gina finished school and Lil John takes very good care of his child. They live together and Gina doesn't want for nothing. Lil John and Corey are getting money in the streets. They dropped out of high school and turned to the streets. I really don't know why they choose to do that because both of them come from loving homes. They had both of their parents in the home that worked and provided for them. I guess they wanted the fast life and fast money.

"Where my girl at?"Lil John asked.
"She's over at the park with Mimi."I said.

Lil John called Gina from his cell phone as if I was lying. We all stood back and watched him. He was always down her back. I'm surprised that Gina is even outside today. Corey was talking on the phone as well. I was ear hustling listening to his conversation. He was talking to his girlfriend Mya. I couldn't stand Mya she was an uppity bitch that thought she was all that because she lived in the suburbs. I wanted to make the bitch mad so I started calling Corey's name out loud in the background.

"Corey, can you buy your sister something to eat? I'm hungry."I said.

Corey ignored me and started explaining to Mya that it was me talking to him. I snickered and Whitney shook her head. I didn't give a fuck. That bitch wasn't going to do shit. I loved making Mya mad. She didn't like me or the fact that Corey and I were play sister and brother. So every chance that I got I pissed her off and rubbed it in her face. Corey ended his phone call.

"What do you all want to eat?"Corey asked.

"Pizza is cool. You can order two large pizza's for the all of us."

Corey agreed and I ordered the pizzas with his phone. Mya had called him on the other line and I answered.

"Hello!"I said with an attidude.

"Can I speak to Corey?"Mya asked.

"Call him back I said."

I hung up and called the pizza place back. Mya called back several times but I didn't click over. When I was done I gave Corey back his phone.

"Here you go; they said the pizzas will be ready in thirty minutes."

I passed Corey his phone and it started to ring. I know it was Mya. I can hear her screaming and cursing in the background. He was explaining and apologizing to her. I was acting like I was engaged in a conversation with Whitney and Lil John when Corey hung up his phone.

"Why you didn't tell me that Mya called back sis? She was screaming in my ear and shit."

"Oh my fault I forgot just that fast."I lied.

"You didn't forget shit."Corey said. We all walked over to the park to join Gina and Hope. Thirty minutes later Corey and Lil John went to pick up the pizzas. We went back to my house to eat and chill under the air conditioner.

Chapter Two

I stood in the bedroom mirror checking myself out before I left out for work. I admired my curves. I was a bad chick in my eyes. I was brown skin, short, and thick. I needed to hurry up and get myself a car. My mother said that she would match whatever I bring to the table. I was standing at the bus stop on my way to work. The bus was running late as usual. I know my boss was going to be upset with me. I could never make it to work on time no matter how early I left out. Needless to say I strolled in my job fifteen minutes late. I worked at a local clothing store in the neighborhood.

Hassan was the owner and the boss. He was a twenty five year old Arab. He was fine and had Arab money. I can tell by the look on his face that he was mad. I tried not to make eye contact with him and start working. It was tax season and very busy. Everyone was spending their tax money. By the end of the day I made so much money off commission. I was making my last sell before Hassan called me to the back to speak with me. "Chiquita I need to speak with you.

"I prepared myself for the lectured I knew it was coming. I walked in the back.

"Yes Hassan you wanted to see me?"

"Yes, Chiquita I want to talk about you being late. You can not continue being late or else I would have to replace you young lady."

"I'm sorry I tried my best to get here on time but the bus is always running late. I would leave out much earlier."

Hassan let me off with a warning. I was happy that I didn't get fired. I needed my job until something else better came along and plus I needed money to buy a car. On the bus ride back home I was thinking about enrolling in school and picking up a trade. I didn't know what I really wanted to do. Gina was going to school for Medical Billing and Coding. Whitney was in school as well. She was going for Criminal Justice and she worked part time at the mall. Hope didn't work. She was turning eight teen in another month and from there she would receive her own government check. She didn't plan on doing too much of nothing with her life. I was time for me to get off the bus. I decided to give Gina a call to see if she was up late and what she was doing. My phone starting ringing and I looked at the screen and noticed it was Chiquita. I pressed the ignore button. I thought it was Lil John calling me back. He was still out in the streets. The last time that I've seen or heard from him was three hours ago when he picked me up from school. I know he was out there making money and trying to provide for me and Mimi. I wasn't working so someone had to pay the bills. Lil John and I have been rocking since the sixth grade. He has been the only men that I've been with. When I became pregnant everyone thought it was the end of the world. They didn't think anything good was going to come out of it. Well someone good did come out of it. My daughter

Mystique aka Mimi; Lil John has been there for the both of us since she was born. We stay in a two bedroom apartment in a pretty good section of the hood. I worried when Lil John was out in the streets with Corey. Corey was cool but he had a lot of enemies and didn't really get along with too many people. Lil John was the opposite and people often warned him about Corey. I called his phone again and this time he picked up. I could hear loud music in the background and could tell that he has been drinking.

"Hello why the hell you aren't picking up your phone? I know damn well you see me calling you!"

"My fault baby I had the music up loud and I didn't hear my phone ring."

"Okay so why haven't you called to check on me and Mimi?"

"I was meaning too, but I got busy baby. I'm on my way home now."

"Yeah ok you better be. You cool you need anything?"Lil John asked.

"What I need is for your ass to be in the house!"

Cool baby I'm on my way in now."

"Okay I love you baby."I said.

"I love you too babe."

"Sneaky Pussy", Coming Soon!

Made in the USA
Lexington, KY
02 February 2017